YOUNG CAPTAIN NEMO
THE SERPENT'S NEST

JASON HENDERSON

Feiwel and Friends
New York

For Katarina, who makes imagining look easy

A FEIWEL AND FRIENDS BOOK
An imprint of Macmillan Publishing Group, LLC
120 Broadway, New York, NY 10271

mackids.com

Our books may be purchased in bulk for promotional, educational, or business use.
Please contact your local bookseller or the Macmillan Corporate and Premium Sales
Department at (800) 221-7945 ext. 5442 or by email at
MacmillanSpecialMarkets@macmillan.com.

Library of Congress Cataloging-in-Publication Data
Names: Henderson, Jason, 1971– author.
Title: The serpent's nest / Jason Henderson.
Description: First edition. | New York : Feiwel and Friends, 2021. | Series: Young
Captain Nemo ; [3] | Audience: Ages 9–13. | Audience: Grades 4–6. | Summary: "In
the third and final installment of this action-packed middle grade series, a twelve-year-
old descendant of Jules Verne's famous antihero must face down giant sea serpents and
solve a centuries old mystery, armed only with his wits, his friends, and his Nemotech
submarine"— Provided by publisher.
Identifiers: LCCN 2020019860 | ISBN 9781250173270 (hardcover)
Subjects: CYAC: Adventure and adventurers—Fiction. | Submarines (Ships)—Fiction.
| Underwater exploration—Fiction. | Science fiction.
Classification: LCC PZ7.H37955 Se 2021 | DDC [Fic]—dc23
LC record available at https://lccn.loc.gov/2020019860

First edition, 2021
Book design by Trisha Previte
Feiwel and Friends logo designed by Filomena Tuosto
Printed in the United States of America by LSC Communications,
Harrisonburg, Virginia

1   3   5   7   9   10   8   6   4   2

PROLOGUE

ON THE PIER that Cora liked to watch, children ran to and fro. What would it be like to run with them?

Cora Land drove her little two-person craft toward the surface of the Atlantic Ocean and felt a tingle of anticipation as the sunlight flickered up ahead. She pulled back on the stick, then ran a finger across the screen in front of her, and the rear engines rumbled as the nose of the craft leveled off. The little craft rose until the water separated over the thick, clear canopy around her. She floated in the craft with her head and shoulders just barely visible, and looked with anticipation across the choppy waves.

There they were! On a great pier that jutted out from a set of cliffs—she had heard all about piers even if they were completely off-limits—dryland people ambled and laughed, moving in every direction. No one seemed to be in a hurry, but some of them—especially the children—ran as if joy pushed them to it.

Cora tapped a button on the menu that floated in the air before her, then slid her goggles up on her head. A portion of the cockpit canopy warped and magnified, and she watched a little girl sit down at the edge of the pier. Early morning sunlight dappled the girl's shoulders as she took bites from a large food of some kind, a pink, tissue-thin cloud that she picked and bit. Behind the little girl, a great building at the top of the pier shone with domes and windows.

Cora sat back and watched dreamily. After a moment, a pair of adults wandered by and reached out their hands and the girl got up, and they wandered again into the crowd of people.

She picked a different group to follow now, a pair of men carrying large cases who were fumbling around with them, until one of them popped his case open and pulled out a guitar. One of her ancestors had brought a guitar with him when he left to follow the ways of her people. She wondered if the drylanders played any differently.

The two men both had their instruments out now and started to play, turning their backs to her, their heads bobbing, maybe singing.

She could almost hear the guitars.

Cora dove the little ship and moved closer to the pier, hidden by the waves. The pier's columns were enormous and made of iron, which seemed to her to be as old as the City. As she grew closer, she saw fish darting around the barnacles—old shellfish that calcified and stuck to structures in the water—on the great columns, which soared from the silt below up past the surface. Once, she knew, her people had walked on this pier, moved among these columns, right here. She had flown her craft past the beaches of Normandy and the cliffs of Maine, but the special thing about the pier at Penarth, Wales, was that the City had started here. Here!

There had been a moment when the people of the City were among those drylanders she loved to watch, and then a moment later—poof. They were gone.

The earpiece in her goggles went *bloop* and she heard a voice: "Cora, where are you?" It was Nils. He was as close to family as she had now, and he looked after her, or at least made sure to check in on her. But he was also the leader of the pilots, and he could be strict.

She brought the earpiece down but left the goggles at her forehead, watching the dryland people wave and smile in the sunlight. "*Bluefin* just got new elevators," she said. That was the little craft's name. "I'm taking it out to see how they do. This ship was having problems, remember?" All that had the extra benefit of being true.

Nils paused and she could picture him, probably in the hangar supervising work on one of the other craft. She could picture her "big brother" looking up, his eyes searching to decide whether to warn her not to go near land. Did he know that she did this—that she did this all the time? Whether they were off the coast of Wales or Hong Kong, did he know that she would go out and just *watch* as the dryland people lived their lives in real air, real sunlight? Scraped their knees on dryland docks and buried one another in the sand? Made sandcastles?

"I don't see you on the scopes," Nils said.

Cora felt nervous now. She didn't want to lie. "There might be a problem with the homing. I'll get it looked at when I'm back." That was also true. Their ships were perfectly built to deflect sonar and other ways drylanders had of seeing craft in the water, but it meant they needed their own homing systems to constantly chirp at one another. This one *might* have a problem because she *might* have *accidentally* turned it off.

"You should head back," Nils said. "It'll be luncheon soon and my mom loves having you."

Cora knew that, but her heart swelled to hear it anyway. She loved Nils's white-haired mother, Delia, who had been around long enough to have built many of the great creations of the City, and now made her feel at home whenever Nils brought her up. It was like having a grandmother.

Has Delia ever been on land? she wondered.

Cora took one last look at the pier and said, "Okay. Headed back." She pulled her goggles on, which caused a colorful, semitransparent menu to float along the bottom and periphery of her vision. She snapped the windshield back to its normal magnification and sighed as she dropped the craft farther. Light green water flowed around her as she sank.

A group of drylanders came into view in swatches of blue and red. As Cora gently moved closer, magnifying the image in her goggles this time, she saw five people diving around the columns. There were two men and three women among them, gesturing to one another with their arms as they floated around one of the iron columns, practicing descending and ascending in the water. They wore thick suits in various colors, with flashing silver tubes strapped to their backs and hoses and cords attached to their mouths. For breathing.

She slowed and watched them All this was familiar to her from her own life—the equipment was different, but she had spent more hours than she could count outside the City, practicing moving in water. But it still struck her as strange that drylanders wanted to leave the warmth of the sun.

She was about to turn away when something caught her eye and she magnified again. One of the men who wore red was floating near a nest of barnacles on the column, and as he swept his arm to point at some yellow fish that passed, a cord from his diving apparatus looped itself around some barnacles. Cora saw it before he did.

The man started to move, and his body jerked. In surprise he whipped around, looking for whatever had trapped him.

"Reach out slowly and lift it off," Cora said aloud, although of course no one could hear her. She gasped as the man didn't do that at all; as he spun, he tightened the cord and got tangled even more.

Cora could feel the man's emotions shift as she saw him start to thrash. For a moment his breathing device jerked out of his mouth and he yanked for it, popping it back in. Another cord looped around the barnacles. He was struggling.

This was bad. She didn't know how drylander diving equipment worked, but if he panicked, his situation would go from bad to worse. He could start breathing too fast and waste his oxygen, or he could rupture his hoses and then maybe even drown.

She throttled the engines of the *Bluefin* and pushed forward even as she knew Nils would say she shouldn't. Absolutely shouldn't. They were secret. She wasn't even supposed to be out here watching people—who did that? No one, that was who. No one except Cora Land.

But she was going to do it anyway.

Cora sent out a call in the water to warn them, a whistle like a whale's, *whee-oooo-pop-pop-pop*, burbling outside the craft as she moved toward the columns of the pier.

Two of the swimmers turned as she became visible, coming closer. She had a brief desire to wave and then thought better of it, hitting a button to make the canopy opaque to them, just a gray mass over the shiny blue hull.

Cora reviewed the menu of options floating before her

and tapped a button labeled CLAWS. The front of the ship shuddered as a metallic hatch opened under the nose, and the right grabber claw shot out. The claw, about a foot and a half wide and shining on the end of a thick cable, soared through the water. Cora controlled it with a joystick display that was only visible through her goggles.

The man was thrashing enough that she had to aim carefully not to hit him with the claw. She wouldn't be able to lift out his hoses—she'd surely break them. So she went for the barnacles instead, slipping one part of the claw under an outcropping and pulling.

Cora felt resistance as the claw grabbed on to the barnacles. Once she had a solid hold, she pressed RETRACT, 100 percent power. She imagined that the whole nest would probably pop away.

But it didn't. She'd underestimated the resistance, and when she hit RETRACT, the cable whined, the *Bluefin* lurched, and the claw snapped right off.

As she watched in horror, the claw sank like a stone while the man continued to struggle. She had made it worse. Now they were afraid, and she hadn't helped at all.

Try again. Don't panic.

Cora launched the left claw, more carefully this time, latching on to a long clump of barnacles. This time she dialed the retraction power down to 25 percent. It began to pull. The craft tilted again, groaning. She throttled the engines, pushing back as the cable slowly pulled. She felt something start to give. Cora increased the power, just a little, 33 percent. Pulling. The barnacles started to slightly separate from the column. The man struggling now seemed to see what she was doing because he reached for the hoses, lifting them.

She increased another 10 percent and watched with satisfaction as the main structure of barnacles crumbled, a huge portion pulling free.

The man swam away from the column, one of the others putting their arms on his shoulders. They began to swim away from the column. But they were staring toward her. What did she look like to them?

She let the barnacles drop and retracted the good claw, then dipped and began to drive the *Bluefin* away. She dove deeper, adrenaline rushing through her body. They had seen her. But she had been able to help. That counted more than anything. It had to.

Nils would notice she was taking a long time. And she would have to explain how she lost a claw. No, that wouldn't be a problem, she'd say she was testing it on barnacles and broke it off. That was true.

It was true, but it wasn't the whole truth, because she couldn't tell the whole truth.

Which was that Cora Land loved the drylanders so much that she risked herself and the City by saving people all the time.

1

"IS THIS WHERE it was?" Gabriel Nemo slid out of the captain's chair and stepped toward the curved wall before him. The viewscreen took up almost a third of the wall of the experimental Nemoship *Kekada*'s bridge or command center. The bridge was smaller than Gabriel was used to—about fifteen feet across, circular, with railings for equipment sweeping all the way around, and numerous handles for swivel-out chairs if they were needed. His chair, the captain's chair, sat permanently in the center, with two crew stations behind him. Gabriel ran his fingers through his short black hair and looked back to his left for his friend and helmsman, Peter. "Like, it was right here?"

But Peter wasn't there. Gabriel winced. On the ship he knew and loved, the *Obscure*, the helmsman would be behind him to his left, but aboard this ship, Peter was on Gabriel's right. *I am going to get this.* He spun to the other side and said, "Are we sure?"

"Yep," Peter said, shrugging. The lights of the viewscreen and the rest of the bridge reflected in Peter's glasses below his tousled blond hair. Peter wore the Nemo uniform of long blue pants and a jacket, although Peter's jacket was open to reveal a DANGANRONPA T-shirt underneath. "The sound that was captured and uploaded came from these coordinates." He pointed at the screen. "Right below the pier."

The viewscreen showed what was directly outside: green water lit up by the *Kekada*'s bright floodlights as they swept over the tall iron columns below Penarth Pier on the coast of Wales. The pier was more than a hundred years old, and the iron was black and rusted, encrusted with barnacles and swarming with fish that flickered colorfully in and out of the floodlights. They were investigating a strange report, one that Gabriel thought might help solve a mystery that kept him up at night. A report that had come from near Tiger Bay, which Gabriel hoped would prove a theory he alone believed.

"And it wasn't just the sound," Peter said.

"Right," Gabriel agreed. "Misty..."

He started to turn right. *No, left. Left for Misty.* He would get it. He looked left to see a tall girl with mountains of thick brown curls, loose strands of them spilling over her face. "What did they say?"

Misty lifted a tablet from a slot before her and flicked it with her hand. "Okay, it's from three weeks ago." She was looking at social media posts from a woman who taught scuba diving near Penarth Pier and around the Bristol Channel, the large body of water ships used to reach Cardiff, Wales. Misty cleared her throat. "Here, uh, blah blah blah . . . '*You won't believe it but I'm writing it here anyway. When Greg*—' that's a scuba student, a tourist '—*got stuck on the pilings below the pier, we were running out of options. And then something like a boat or even like a plane, I don't know which, came out of nowhere and broke the mass of barnacles his gear was stuck on. They did it with a cable and a sort of grabber claw. Maybe the navy? I'm asking around. The claw grabbed on to the barnacles and pulled. I could hear an engine whining and a fierce crack, and the cable broke, and as soon as it did another cable came and took its place and started pulling. Finally the barnacles broke, and Greg was free—and they disappeared. I didn't get a good look at them. Mostly just the cable and claw, and the vessel itself was back about twenty feet, and hard to see in the murky water.*'"

Gabriel pointed at the mass of barnacles. "I can totally see how you could get your gear stuck on that if you weren't careful. That would be pretty scary for a beginner." He pictured it. A guy goes on a dive, he comes in close to the iron poles to take a picture, and one of the straps of his gear gets snagged on the spiny rocks. And then he can't come up and starts to panic. Gabriel could almost feel the

11

man's fear. "So a mysterious rescuer shows up. Out of the sea and into it again."

"And not for the first time," Misty said. Ever since the crew had started looking into the Bristol Channel, they had found many such mysterious rescues up and down the coast.

"But this time we have the video the lady posted," Peter said. "I mean, it's black and doesn't show anything, but it has the sound and the location marker, which is *here*."

"Let's hear the sound again," Gabriel said.

Peter nodded and tapped a button.

"Here you go."

A strange sound emanated from the speakers, distant and crackling. It whined like a high-pitched song, almost like a whale. It bleated and popped, *whee-oooo-pop-pop-pop*. Beyond that was a distinct engine whine unlike any craft Gabriel had ever heard.

Peter sat back, staring at the ceiling as he listened. "I hear something like a…like a *gurgle* in there, like water running through machinery. It's pretty strange."

"*Definitely* not navy," Misty said.

"Totally not," agreed Peter.

The *Kekada* rumbled, its stabilizers steadying them.

"I think it's them," Gabriel said. The hair on the back of his neck prickled.

"It's Maelstrom," Peter said. Maelstrom was an organization that used a whole navy of private submarines all over the world. They were criminals, though.

"Rescuers coming from the sea. Here, at Tiger Bay. With this mysterious equipment."

Peter leaned back his head and sang, *"Maaaaaeeeellstrommm."* He sat forward. "Just because you have this crazy theory…"

"I don't know about crazy," Misty offered. "Maybe a little…"

Gabriel wondered what Misty was about to say. *Overhopeful? Naive?*

"He doesn't need you to defend him," Peter said with a grin, and looked back at Gabriel. "…this crazy theory, let's say it out loud, that the survivors of the actual Nemoship *Nautilus* are now running around Great Britain playing *underwater Batman.* Which I guess is Aquaman, but you get me."

Gabriel held up his hands. "I know."

"It's like Bigfoot with you," Peter said. "And I'm into it. I am. But you know, most of the time when someone sees Bigfoot? It's a gorilla."

"Well it's not a gorilla and it's not any navy," Gabriel said. "And it's not us."

Peter looked at Misty. "So it's Maelstrom, am I right?"

Misty shrugged. "A gang like Maelstrom doing anonymous rescues? *Aliens* would be more likely."

"It's not aliens. Anyway, at least we know they were here," Gabriel said.

Gabriel looked over at a small Nemoglass rack on the shelf under the viewscreen. Suspended between two clear poles was a golden pin about seven inches long. There was engraving on it that he couldn't read from here, but that he had looked at countless times. ALL HANDS TO THE TIGERS.

It was a message left by the crew of the Nemoship *Nautilus* before they disappeared more than a hundred years ago.

Tigers. There was only one place that a mariner was likely to mean in 1910. Tiger Bay, the busy seaport now known as *Cardiff* Bay, just a couple of miles from the cliffs where they floated right now.

Had the *Nautilus* crew gone to land? Had they shipwrecked aboard a different craft, sunk to their dooms? Or, as Gabriel suspected, had they disappeared into the sea with a *purpose*? The knowledge and technology of the Nemos gave them options not available to any regular crew.

Gabriel had intended to wait until the winter holidays to begin their search of Tiger Bay and its surroundings for any sign of the crew. But then in late October, they found the posting about the strange rescue, which led to more stories—until he developed his new theory. The *Nautilus* crew was alive. Descendants of them, anyway. And they were active. He thought about it day and night, talked about it at lunch incessantly.

Then he hit upon an opportunity. There was a break coming up, this *Thanksgiving* thing, whatever it was. The perfect opportunity to go look for clues. They could take out the experimental ship *Kekada* that they were using after the loss of the *Obscure*.

His mom, who was teaching at the Nemo Institute where he and his crew went to school, thought this was a great plan, so he had been surprised when his crew had a different reaction.

"You want us to skip *Thanksgiving*?" Misty had said.

She put down her sandwich and stared across the cafeteria table. "Are you joking?"

"I dunno, man," Peter said. He was next to Misty and looked at him over a plate piled high with chili dogs.

Peter picked up a chili dog with one hand, angling it so the chili drizzled away from him. "This is the West Coast. We're here." He held up a can of Coke with his other hand, keeping it far away from the chili dog. "Wales is in the United Kingdom. Waaaay over here. So we'd have to go down through Panama and up across the Atlantic."

Gabriel chuckled. "I know what the globe looks like."

"That's good. Have you forgotten how *big* it is? That's like seventy-five hundred miles. Even with the new drive it's like a full day just to get there, with slowing down through the canal." The *Kekada* was a modular ship that allowed the Nemos to plug in all sorts of experiments, so they had been quick to add one of the SC drives that Peter himself had invented. SC stood for "supercavitation," and it enabled a submarine to move as fast as a plane.

"Okay, so it's a long way," Gabriel agreed. "But we have a week off. We can find them!"

"Find your urban legend, you mean?"

"Not when Thursday is *Thanksgiving*," Misty interrupted.

Gabriel held up his hands. "Right, okay, what is this Thanksgiving thing?"

Misty smiled, but her eyes were a little hurt. Like she was patiently explaining something to a toddler who had punched her in the nose. "This *thing*... is a holiday, and it's important. Our parents aren't going to just let us skip it to go to Wales. They'll want us with them. I mean, I want to be with them. I barely get to see my sister as it is." Just this school year Misty and Peter had begun attending the Nemo Institute, just over the horizon from their homes in Santa Marta, California. Gabriel understood Misty's pain—he had spent months living in California alone with his parents at Nemolab at the bottom of the ocean.

"She's right, Gabe. Thanksgiving is no small thing." Peter took a bite out of the chili dog that had stood for California. "My mom pretends we're back in the sticks and she makes enough food to feed North Carolina. She'll want me there."

"I get that it's an American thing and they don't do Thanksgiving at the bottom of the ocean," Misty said. "But trust us on this."

"O-okay." Gabriel looked down at his seaweed wrap and poked at it with a soy fry. So this Thanksgiving holiday was important to them. He could work with that. "Well...I mean, what if we *all* go?"

The three looked at one another in silence for a moment and then Misty and Peter started to nod.

Below Penarth Pier, Gabriel stared at the iron columns. "Well, we'll keep looking."

"Did the post say the first cable broke?" Peter asked.

"Right." Misty looked at the report. "First one broke, then they tried again."

"If the rescuers don't want to be seen, that's pretty brave," Gabriel observed. "To break some equipment and keep trying. Everything they try gives more time to be watched."

"If equipment broke, maybe they left something behind," Peter suggested.

"Yeah," Gabriel said. "How much time do we have?"

"It's four fifteen," Misty said. "We're supposed to meet everyone at five."

Gabriel nodded. Okay. They had promised to join the families—Peter's mom and Misty's parents and sister—for a whole slew of activities. "Just a quick sweep. Take a look at the floor."

Peter took the joystick in front of him in hand, and the whole of the *Kekada* tilted. On the viewscreen, the floodlights swept down the posts to the silty floor of the bay. He tapped buttons on the tablet in front of him and reversed the ship.

A portion of the screen next to the camera image showed a diagram of the *Kekada* as it moved, and Gabriel watched it tilt back, facing downward as it scuttled backward.

Scuttled was the right word. Unlike the fishlike *Obscure*, the *Kekada* was about forty feet wide, tapered on each end, with a wide, flat, black face at the front covered in cameras and lights. Their ship looked like a crab, and in fact that was what *Kekada* meant in Hindi.

The floor swirled with grayish white silt and tiny fish and detritus. "There's the broken barnacles," Gabriel said as the light swept across a pile of jagged, cementlike broken bits.

"I don't see anything like equipment," Misty said. As they moved along at about two yards of lit-up silt at a time, nothing man-made showed.

"No, but we're on the right track. We just don't have time," Gabriel said.

"We can come back," Misty offered. "Try again tomorrow?"

Peter snapped his fingers. "How about we try sonar?"

"All it'll see is the pier," Gabriel said.

Peter flipped on the sonar anyway, and half the screen was taken up by a blue set of circles in circles. They heard a quiet *beep* as a bright line on the sonar screen began to sweep around the center. Within a moment the shape of the pier appeared before them, the iron beams showing as large masses. "Here," Peter said, touching the tablet, and the speakers erupted with crackles and high-pitched rhythmic pinging sounds. "Normally we don't actually listen to the sonar's *sound*, we just look at the shapes it makes on the screen. But listen to this."

Peter got up and went to stand by Gabriel near the screen and pointed as the sonar hand moved from empty sea to cross past the beams of the pier. "Hear that? The sound gets deeper as it bounces off the columns. Different things make different sounds when we bounce sound off them. If we were to go up fifty feet there'd be all this noise from boats running around on the surface. But it's pretty quiet down here. So it might work."

"What might work?" Gabriel asked.

Peter went back to his seat and pulled the joystick, and Gabriel shifted his weight as the bridge tilted and spun around. "We sweep the floor. If anything metal has been dropped and it's anywhere nearby, we can find it."

On the screen, the image of the *Kekada* tilted down again as the sonar pinged out and came back. "Silt. Silt."

A rough, lower sound came back, and on the screen a shape about a yard long and a foot wide showed. "What's that?" Gabriel asked.

They moved closer, the floodlights revealing a long,

square shape. Part of it was covered by silt, but Gabriel sighed when they saw it fully. "It's a log. Probably left over from one of the original piers."

"Okay," Misty said. "But—guys. We know this works; we can come back tomorrow and pick up where we left off."

A strange, high-pitched *ping* came back as the sonar screen swept again. As they moved past the log, the ping rose in its tone. Gabriel looked on the sonar screen.

"We got something," Peter said. The *Kekada* moved along the floor, the floodlights leaving the log behind.

Ping.

On the sonar screen, a new shape appeared on the floor. It was an irregular lump.

The floodlights came to rest on a mound of silt. A slight glimmer reflected at the top, like a coiled snake whose nose was barely pressing out from a blanket of dust.

"It's metal." Peter's voice rose like the sonar ping.

Gabriel looked at Misty. "I know about the time. Do we have time to get out and look at this?"

Before Misty could answer, Peter brought up a different screen. "Hang on, I'll use one of the arms."

Underneath the *Kekada*, eight jointed robot legs with claws at the end were nestled snugly in a recess of the ship's hull. The arms lit up bright blue on the diagram on the viewscreen as Peter brought them online.

Peter grabbed a joystick. On the viewscreen, the metal hand of the arm emerged from below, its silver claw open and hunting, as if following a scent. The joints moved as the clawed arm gingerly stretched toward the shape in the silt.

"Tap it," Gabriel said. "Just a little."

Peter nodded and jiggled the joystick, and the claw on the end of the arm touched the pyramid-shaped thing. Silt fell away from the nose.

It wasn't a nose. It was a metal claw, almost like theirs. It lay at the top of a coiled cable, the end of which extended from the coil in frayed bits of wire and metal.

Gabriel bobbed on his heels. "It's a cable claw. Just like they said. It's them. It's *them*!"

"Well, it's someone," Peter said. Then he murmured a singsong "*Maelstrom.*"

"Whatever." He looked over at Misty. "Grab it. Let's put it in the hold. We can look at it above."

Peter used the *Kekada*'s grappling arm to grasp the damaged claw and lift it off the floor. They heard scraping against the hull as the robot arm dragged the treasure toward the aft of the *Kekada*. Then another mechanical sound as the door to a collecting trunk opened up, and a heavy *thunk* as Peter dropped their find into the trunk. The trunk shut with another heavy sound.

"Not bad." Misty went over to Peter's station with a hand up, which Peter slapped in a high five.

"Not bad at *all*," Gabriel said. They'd have to get topside to get the thing out of the trunk and look at it. He was aching to get to it. "That's the first physical—"

A new sound then pinged off the sonar. Gabriel looked at the screen. Something came across the edge of the sweep, a shape, a craft, small. Peter instantly tapped a button and the speakers emanated a sound: a strange, high-pitched whine of an engine. Nothing Gabriel recognized at all.

"What is that?" Misty asked.

The sound dropped away completely as the sonar hand moved, and when it came around again, the shape was gone.

"Increase the range. Level off."

The *Kekada*'s nose rose and Peter said aye, and more concentric circles appeared on the sonar.

Nothing. The shape had been there. A craft had come close. Close enough for them to pick it up as they were concentrating on a circle about seventy feet wide. But nothing now.

"They watched us," Gabriel said, the hairs on the back of his neck prickling. "Guys, they watched us grab their claw."

"It was at sixty-five degrees from our position," Misty said.

"Right. Peter?"

The *Kekada* spun around and Gabriel grabbed on. The sonar swept as they began to move.

But the shape and the sound were gone.

"We could chase them." Peter looked up. "How fast can anyone move?"

"Peter—"

"That was the *sound*," Peter said.

Gabriel saw Misty's eyes, the same hurt as when he'd called Thanksgiving a *thing*. "Uh. No. We have an appointment."

He went and sat in his chair.

Contact, he thought. They had made contact.

Is it you?

"We're gonna be late. Let's head in."

"Aye, aye," Peter said. He turned the *Kekada* toward the pier.

2

PETER BROUGHT THE *Kekada* up to the surface at Penarth Pier, just barely. As Gabriel climbed out the top hatch, the only part sticking above the water was a few inches of sloped, burnished red metal. The rest of the ship was mostly hidden under the waves, and the overcast skies worked with the shadows under the pier to conceal them. Gabriel saw some craft in the distance, the nearest vessel being a fishing boat half a mile away. The sounds of merry-go-round music and the distant chatter of crowds filtered down from the boardwalk, sixty feet above where the *Kekada* sat.

Misty stuck her head up and started to climb out, saying, "We need to hurry."

"You bet, but can you give me a hand with the collecting

trunk?" Gabriel's feet splashed as they walked down the hull toward the tail of the crablike ship. They stopped at a visible rectangle of seams and Misty knelt down, putting her hand against a sensor. It lit up with a blue shimmer, recognizing her hand as that of a crewmember. Gabriel felt the dull *thunk* of fasteners unlocking.

Gabriel looked back toward the top hatch as Peter emerged and called, "Peter, could you raise the stern about six inches?"

Peter put his hand on an iron ladder running along the rusty column of the pier and nodded. He had water splashing on his shoes. He pulled a silver controller from his jacket pocket, which he could use to run the *Kekada* nearly as well as if he'd been sitting at the helm. "Raising," he called. Gabriel felt the ship tilt, and the back half of the *Kekada* rose, water flowing away. The red hull sparkled with droplets.

Misty looked back at Peter's feet and whispered, "Can you believe it? Three months ago he'd never have dared to stand in water."

That was true. Peter, the helmsman of a submarine, was afraid of water. But ever since he had been forced to command the Nemoship *Obscure* alone and escape out the hatch as it flooded, he had been noticeably more comfortable with situations that used to terrify him. When Gabriel had met the genius boy from his mechanics class, Peter had been so afraid of water that his throat would close up if he tried to drink it. Now he could stand in it. Gabriel reckoned that Peter wasn't about to go swimming on purpose any time soon, but the change was amazing anyway.

Gabriel grabbed a handle on one end of the rectangle and Misty grabbed another, and they slid the three-foot box out easily. But it was heavy—they grunted as they lifted it up, because even though the metal was light, it was full of water. Gabriel looked down and flipped open a drain on his end, then Misty found hers, and water poured out onto the hull. After a moment the trunk was only weighted by the strange treasure inside.

They hauled the trunk back to the ladder.

Peter began to climb. "Sink the crab?" he asked.

Gabriel grabbed on to the ladder and went up a few rungs behind Peter. The trunk was light enough that he could let it hang by one handle in his hand, though he kept it out of the way of the ladder, lest he accidentally drop it on Misty's head. "Sink the crab."

Misty started to climb the ladder below as Peter worked the remote. The iris of the top hatch closed and submerged with the rest of the craft, and for a moment all three of them watched the *Kekada* disappear from view, moving off and down to the floor of the bay.

Then they climbed quickly, hopping out onto the boardwalk at the top. There were plenty of tourists around the pier, and a silver-haired couple in matching red windbreakers waved at them as Misty took one end of the trunk.

Seagulls cried all about them, landing on the posts and diving toward the sea.

"Catch anything?" the man said, smiling as he indicated the metal trunk.

Gabriel wondered what they looked like exactly, wearing their matching uniforms. "Sunken treasure," Misty said, running her free hand through her mountain of hair.

The couple laughed and ambled toward the end of the dock as the crew kept walking toward the street. "How much time do we have?" Gabriel asked.

"Twenty minutes," Misty said as they entered the shadow of Penarth Pier Pavilion. It was the jewel of the pier right at the entrance, a wooden concert hall with latticework, ornate windows, and four towers, one at each corner, each with a lovely powder-blue dome at the top. A man was handing out flyers for upcoming concerts as students and families bought snacks from a variety of booths.

"Oh!" Peter ran past Misty and Gabriel. "We gotta get some cotton candy."

"We call it candy floss, my American friend," the woman behind the cotton candy booth said. She handed Peter a paper cone piled a yard high with pink sugar as Peter produced some bills from the inside breast pocket of his uniform jacket. As she handed the candy floss over, the woman looked him up and down. "What's that uniform? Are you in the Scouts?"

"Nemoship," Peter said. "We scour the bottom of the

sea for bad guys and monsters." The woman laughed heartily. Peter turned to Gabriel with the cotton candy. "You want some?"

"We're gonna do dinner after the tour, do we need candy?"

"Like that's an answer. I've already got candy *on me.* I just want...more. Misty?"

"Ye-yes but we have to hurry." She grabbed a piece of the candy floss with one hand and folded it into her mouth as she brought out her cell. Gabriel saw her bringing up a car-calling app.

Gabriel scanned the street as they walked to the front of the pier and saw the posts where Ubers and Lyfts and British taxicabs picked up and dropped off their passengers.

"It's three miles to—" She looked into the door of a car as it pulled up. "Is this car for Misty?" After a brief back and forth, they hopped in.

"Mermaid Quay," Peter said, pronouncing it with a hard *A,* like *day.*

"It's *kee,*" Misty said. *Quay* was pronounced like *key* and was a large bunch of buildings at the mouth of a body of water. Mermaid Quay was where they were to meet their families for a boat tour of Cardiff Bay. Gabriel wished that since they had already been in the ocean, they could have piloted the *Kekada* straight into and through Cardiff Bay to the meeting place, but there was no way for a ship as wide as theirs to get through the entry point to the bay. And even if they could fit, he didn't want the kind of attention they would surely draw.

"Either way, mate," the driver said. "I can get you there."

In the quick trip from the pier to the quay, Gabriel couldn't help being obsessed by their find. He ran his hand along the trunk, which sat between him and Misty. He flipped a lever and lifted back the long metal lid. In what little water remained in the trunk, the strange silver cable coiled, its robotic claw lying open. "Would you look at this thing?"

"Yeah, yeah," Misty said. "We're gonna park in just a second."

"We've gotta *study* this." The car was coming to a stop at a circular drive where more tourists crowded up and down the block. The enormous lake that was Cardiff Bay flashed and glimmered beyond the buildings.

"Thanks!" Misty said as she reached over Gabriel to pop open the door. "We will look at it. After the tour."

"Do you think I could, like, wait for you guys?" Gabriel looked down at the claw.

"Don't even think about it," Misty said. "You're here for family."

Gabriel sighed and closed the trunk. He got out, carrying it by both handles until Misty took the other end.

They walked into the crowd and past a tall Ferris

wheel. Even in late November, with the sky gray and the temperature in the mid-forties, the place had the feel of high summer. Voices chattered everywhere amidst the clanking of boat lines as they headed toward the marina.

Someone waved wildly from a crowd of about fifty people next to a long white boat that bobbed up and down in the water at a landing. As they drew closer they saw it was Ms. Kosydar, Peter's mom, with her giant glasses and dark blond hair. Next to her, Misty's parents and eight-year-old sister, Molly, were waiting. Molly had her own enormous cotton candy.

Misty and Peter took the lead and picked up the pace, carrying Gabriel along as he was still on the other end of the trunk. As they sat the trunk down, Misty threw her arms around her sister. Peter's mom went in for the hug and then spiraled back as Peter offered a fist bump. Gabriel waved.

"That's our party of seven!" Mr. Jensen, looking smart in a dark sport jacket, called back to a woman with a clipboard.

Molly said, "Dad wasn't sure you were going to make it. What's that?" She pointed at the trunk.

"Sunken treasure," Peter said. "Gold doubloons."

"Really?"

"No, not really," he said, ruffling her hair. "It's a robot claw."

"You're silly," Molly said.

"Just ignore him," Misty said. She and Gabriel picked up the trunk as the crowd began moving onto the boat. It was a white craft about sixty feet long, with a hard roof and windows all along the sides, with seats for two or three like a school bus. The group took up seats in the middle along the port, or left, side. Misty's parents had their own seat up front, while Misty sat behind them with her sister, Molly. Peter was about to sit with his mom, but then flopped down next to Gabriel behind Misty.

"Welcome to the Cardiff Bay Aquacoach," the woman with the clipboard said as she hopped aboard, taking a mic off the wall and speaking into it. She wore blue slacks and a blue vest over a white blouse, with a gold scarf around her neck. Her ID tag said TIFFANEY.

"We're about to take a tour of one of the modern marvels of the world: Cardiff Bay," she said. "We're leaving Mermaid Quay, which you can recognize for the sculpture of the mermaid in the waves and the sculpture of a ship's hull with the face of a sailor lost at sea. *'In Memory of the Merchant Seafarers from the Ports of Barry, Penarth, and Cardiff Who Died in Times of War.'*"

Gabriel looked out at Mermaid Quay as they pulled away from it, the hotels and restaurants receding slowly as the boat rocked. He felt the engines rumble as the captain in his small pilot house up front increased their speed.

"What do you figure, six cylinders?" Peter asked, listening to the engines with his ear tilted toward the floor.

31

Gabriel shrugged. "The Nemos make their own engines." He wasn't as familiar with common engine designs as Peter, who understood anything that used fuel.

"You're traveling aboard a brand-new waterbus built to safely carry sixty passengers," Tiffaney said, "with a six-cylinder Volvo engine capable of speeds of fifty kilometers per hour."

"Boom." Peter pumped his fist.

"Can that speed be right?" Now Misty whispered back to them.

"It'll go forty kilometers tops," Peter whispered.

"I'm trying to listen!" Molly hissed.

"Can anyone tell me what Cardiff Bay used to be called?" Tiffaney asked.

Molly raised her hand. "Tiger Bay!"

"That's right. Once upon a time this was Tiger Bay, where boats came in and went to sea bearing coal, and later iron. A sailor here would run across forty-five different nationalities. But it wasn't always nice—as sailors came in and stayed for a few days they would often get up to mischief and sometimes murder. Cardiff Docks was like the water of the bay itself—busy, dark, sludgy, and dangerous."

Gabriel heard *Cardiff Docks* and looked out at the sparkling blue surface of the freshwater lake and pictured what he had only seen in old photographs: the network of wooden docks and anchored ships, sailors fighting on shore. There would be flashing knives and people making deals by torchlight. And somewhere, a hundred years ago, some-how, the crew of the *Nautilus* had been right nearby.

"In World War II, the docks were extremely busy mov-ing materiel for the Allies, but by 1960, the area was nearly dead. This whole five hundred acres was a marsh where the coal ships no longer came, where sometimes it was mud and sometimes it flooded. And then in the 1980s, the Welsh secretary of state Nicholas Edwards hit upon an idea. We would dam the Ely and Taff Rivers to create this fresh-water lake known as Cardiff Bay."

"Tidal rivers," Gabriel said quietly to Peter and Misty. "That's why it was either mud or flood. The rivers changed as the sea tides came in."

"What they created was *this*," Tiffaney said as the boat neared the other side of the lake and a long concrete bar-rier rose in their view. "They created the dam called Car-diff Barrage."

Peter pointed to the sections of the dam that rose high over the lake. "Look at that thing."

Tiffaney called, "Cardiff Barrage is one-point-one kilometers or point-seven miles long, with three locks for moving ships and boats into the bay."

"What does *locks* mean?" Molly asked. Misty's mom looked back and started to answer, but Molly was looking at Misty, who didn't fail her.

"A lock is like a doorway for boats," Misty said. "See, this lake is always at the same height. The sea might be lower. So you come in from the sea, then you sail into the doorway, and it closes and raises you up by bringing in water. And then when the water is up, the door opens, and you just sail out into the lake."

"The largest lock is ten meters, or thirty-three feet wide," Tiffaney said.

"The *Kekada* wouldn't fit," Peter said.

"Nope," Gabriel said. "But there are other ways."

Peter grinned. "I know, those legs on the *Kekada*, you just wanna climb around something with them, you know?"

The crew had so much technology. And if the Nemos had been able to develop such amazing tech, wouldn't the *Nautilus* crew, with the original Captain Nemo at the helm, have done the same?

The claw in the trunk next to him was practically calling out to him. Gabriel put his hand on the lid. Molly turned toward him and leaned way over her seat back, bracing herself on her skinny arms. "Can I see your sunken treasure?"

"If you don't tell your sister," Peter said.

Gabriel opened the trunk between him and Peter, and Molly leaned farther over to peer into the metal case. Gabriel reached out and steadied her so she wouldn't fall as he took another look himself at the claw in the inch of water.

"Is that writing?" Molly asked as she looked into the trunk. "Look."

Gabriel looked closer and this time saw some tiny

etching on the claw, barely visible under bits of sand and seaweed. He reached in and tilted the artifact, wiping away a smudge of wet sand. "I can't read it."

"Yeah, but it *is* an inscription," Peter said. "You found a clue, Molly." Peter gave Molly a high five.

Misty looked back. "Can we pay attention?"

When Peter nodded at Misty he looked past her, and his eyes grew wide. Gabriel followed his gaze.

"Dude," Peter said, pointing to a system of giant iron gears. "Look at the lock mechanisms. Those must be twenty feet tall."

"Well, sure. It's gotta be strong, the locks have to carry thousands of tons of water."

"To the side of the barrage is the fish pass," Tiffaney said as they moved past a sort of waterfall of concrete, where water came in from the ocean in an undulating spray. "This waterfall allows trout and salmon to enter and leave the lake—and then travel hundreds of miles up and down the Atlantic."

"That would be *thousands* of miles," Misty said quietly. "Especially the trout."

Her mom reached over and gave Misty an affectionate squeeze on the shoulder. Gabriel watched Misty beam, and it was the same happiness that Peter had on his face as he watched the machinery. Gabriel glanced at Ms. Kosydar, who was watching the same equipment intently.

He relaxed. Coming to Cardiff had been his idea, but

the warmth the families brought was a gift he had not expected.

A tiny whistle sounded from Misty's jacket, and after a moment she looked back over the seat again, holding out her phone in the palm of her hand. "Look. This is from today," she said.

MYSTERY RESCUER FROM THE SEA RETURNS, it said.

ALIENS OR MERMAIDS?

Gabriel bent forward to peer at the phone as Peter came shoulder to shoulder to read as well. It was an article from a Cardiff blog.

"'A mysterious person came from the sea in a small craft to save passengers of a pleasure craft who had fallen overboard in a collision with a fishing vessel,'" Peter read. "'The rescuer used mechanical claws…'"

Tiffaney was droning on, but Gabriel wasn't hearing anymore as the three looked at one another.

The strangers were still active. And very soon, he knew he was going to find them.

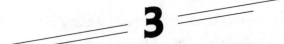

3

"OKAY, NOW I want to get a look at this," Gabriel said, dragging the trunk behind him as they climbed out of the enormous Land Rover that Ms. Kosydar had rented.

"Sure," Peter said. "What's for dinner?" He addressed this generally to the parents, who led the seven up to the door of the cottage they were renting three miles from Penarth Pier. Under the cloudy skies of the early evening, the cottage fairly glowed from its windows. Leaves of ivy covered it.

"Can we have a fire?" Molly asked, and as Mr. Jensen unlocked the front door, Misty rubbed her sister's shoulder and said, "You bet."

As they all moved inside, Misty and Molly went to the fireplace in the living room and immediately started gathering kindling from a copper basket there. The parents went under a little archway that separated the living room from the kitchen and started pulling things out of the refrigerator. "We still need to do Thanksgiving dinner shopping," Ms. Kosydar said.

Peter flopped down on a couch, putting his low-slung Nemotech boots up on the coffee table, just in time for his mom to sing out, "No shoes on the coffee table." When Gabriel looked up, Ms. Kosydar had her head in the refrigerator, so apparently the sound of the shoes alone had been recognizable to her.

Gabriel sat the trunk next to the coffee table and unlatched it. "Okay."

Peter dropped his feet and bent to look into the trunk. Misty wiped her hands as she blew out a long match. The twigs below the logs in the fireplace began to crackle as she came and knelt next to the trunk. The coiled claw lay there, wet and grimy. The claw itself was about two feet long from its wrist—or so Gabriel thought of it, where it attached to the silver cable—to the tips of its pincers.

Gabriel reached in to grab it and Mr. Jensen said, "You might want some paper to put that on. Whatever it is."

Molly brought Misty several newspapers from next to the fireplace and they spread them out. Then Peter and Gabriel lifted the claw from the trunk.

"It's light," Peter said. "It looks like steel, but I guess it's aluminum—or something like it."

Gingerly they laid the claw on the coffee table, where it dripped water onto the newspaper.

"I'm making a list!" Ms. Kosydar called, leaning in the archway. "We need turkey. Cranberry sauce."

"Oh that's right," Gabriel said. "So you . . . eat a bird?"

"You don't *have* to eat a bird," Misty said. "Can you get Gabriel some Tofurkey?"

"And some people go for stuffing." Peter looked up from the claw. "We're really big on stuffing."

"What goes in stuffing?" Gabriel asked.

Misty said, "Well, it used to be bread that they crammed into the actual bird, but generally it's . . . bread and gravy."

"And eggs," Peter said.

"Boiled egg whites," Ms. Kosydar pointed at Peter, nodding. "And celery. Olives."

"And liver," Peter said. "You gotta have liver."

"Turkey liver?" Gabriel grimaced.

"Whatever liver," Peter said. "I mean, I guess you can get tofu liver or something. Is that a thing?"

"You're asking the wrong guy." Gabriel wasn't sure what tofu liver would even taste like, since he had no idea what real liver tasted like. "It's Monday, this dinner you're planning is, what, Thursday?"

"Yes," Peter said solemnly. "Thanksgiving is Thursday. And yes, it will take until then to get ready."

Gabriel shrugged. "Okay." He took a pencil from an end table next to the couch and pushed the claw so that it rocked. The writing where the claw met the cable glistened. "There's Molly's writing."

Misty bent down by the table. She took out her phone and snapped a pic, and then straightened up as she enlarged it.

Carved into the claw was a string of letters:

DN-2-BLUEFIN—R

"*Bluefin*," Gabriel repeated. "Surrounded by *DN-2* and R."

Peter turned the claw over. "We haven't been able to look at Maelstrom's equipment much. So there's no telling. But I'd bet that *Bluefin* is the name of the vessel it came off of."

Misty was already searching on her phone, which had access to the Nemo databases. "We don't have anything on a ship called *Bluefin*."

"We don't know how Maelstrom names their ships," Peter said.

"Or how *they* would," Gabriel countered. By *they* he meant the Nemo descendants.

The aroma of spaghetti sauce began to waft into the living room. "Dinner," their parents called.

"Wait, there's another one," Misty said as she held her phone out to snap a pic of the metal band that ran around the "wrist" of the claw, connecting it to the cable. She enlarged the picture and showed it to them. There were tiny letters in a stylized scrawl.

WIW

"W I W?" Peter looked around. "Anyone?"

Gabriel felt the blood drain from his face, and he held out his hand. Misty handed him the phone. He turned the picture toward them and swiveled it. "It's not W-I-W. It's M-I-M."

"What's that?" Molly asked.

Gabriel had seen it stamped on books his entire life. "MIM stands for *Mobilis in Mobili*. It's Latin for 'change in the changes.'" He brought out his own phone and pulled up a bookmarked item from the Nemo database, then pointed to the letters scrawled in the corner. "It's the motto of the *Nautilus*."

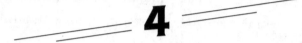

4

SIX HOURS LATER, Gabriel blinked half-awake to the chirp of his Nemotech wristband. He'd laid it on the night table next to the twin bed in the smallest bedroom in the cottage. Above him, a ceiling fan slowly turned, and he lifted his head groggily. A painting glowed faintly in the moonlight. The painting was very old, and Gabriel could make out the image of desperate men in a tiny boat reaching for a sailor who had fallen into the water only to be set upon by an incredible creature. It was a shark but painted by someone who had probably never seen one, a shark with eyelids that Gabriel felt certain had made its way into his dreams.

His wristband chirped again. He sat up, snatching it off the nightstand.

A message meant for the British Coast Guard flickered across the screen in glowing letters. SOS—SHIP IN TROUBLE—UNKNOWN ANIMAL ATTACK—BRISTOL CHANNEL.

Followed by a string of coordinates.

That made no sense. Unknown *animal attack?* Gabriel tried to imagine what sort of animal could put a ship in trouble in the channel. Short of a lion breaking out of its cage on deck, he was at a loss. A whale might give a small boat trouble—though of course it *wouldn't.* Whales didn't attack ships.

Then again, he'd seen some strange things. Gabriel scratched his head and pulled on his blue shirt, glancing again at the weird eyes of the imaginary shark. The Lodgers were big enough to try to *eat* a small ship. They were "unknown animals," too.

But it wouldn't be the Lodgers. Not way over here. His family had made a home for them in a valley about fifty miles from Nemolab, clear on the other side of the Western Hemisphere.

He wanted to call whoever sent the SOS and ask, *Hey! What sort of animal?* But he didn't have their radios. He would need the *Kekada* for that. And he would need his crew.

As he pulled on a pair of uniform pants and his dive boots, he wondered briefly if he would have to go knocking on their doors. He mentally started laying out his path to Peter's room first, then Misty's. Gabriel went to his own bedroom door, stepping softly in the boots. He opened it, expecting to see the dark living room and the potted plants next to the couch.

But two shadows stood at the door already. Misty and Peter were dressed and waiting.

"I wrote a note," Misty's dark silhouette whispered. "Let's go."

Peter handed Gabriel his jacket as they passed the coat rack and whispered, "What the heck is an animal attack on a boat?" His eyes were puffy. But he had gotten up nevertheless.

Misty opened the door and they hustled into the street to unlock their bikes. She shrugged. "It's probably a mistake."

"That's what I'm thinking," Gabriel agreed.

"A whale isn't gonna attack a ship." Peter hopped on his bike and trilled the bell on the handlebar. He winced as the ringing echoed along the cobblestones. "Sorry. Habit."

They pedaled down the dark street, into and out of the circles of light cast down by streetlamps, past ivy-covered cottages like the one they had just left. Soon they were onto the main road, sloping down and picking up speed. Gabriel could see the sparkle of the ocean on the horizon.

"You don't suppose it's the Lodgers?" Misty asked.

"Hunh-uh," Gabriel said. "Can't be."

"Where is this ship?" Misty asked Peter.

"I haven't looked on my phone yet." Peter sat back, pedaling with no hands. "I could figure it out with Google

Maps, but we're headed for the ship anyway. The moment I get in my seat, I'll bring it up."

When they reached Penarth Pier, the structure that by day had been awash in the laughter of tourists and splashing swimmers was dead; the only sounds were the clanging of lines against boat slips and the crashing of surf. They rode their bikes down to the beach right next to the pier. Peter leapt off his bike, dropping it behind him as he yanked a curved, silvery remote out of his jacket pocket. Gabriel took Peter's bike and locked it to a metal pole next to his own and Misty's.

Peter's silhouette was black against what seemed a painted sweep of stars that disappeared into a sparkling ocean. His jacket flapped in the wind. "You gotta admit," he said as the device in his hand lit up, "the *Kekada*'s remote makes this a lot easier. It's something we want to make sure is part of the new . . . whatever the new ship will be called."

When they sailed aboard the *Obscure*—and every time Gabriel thought of it, he ached—they had to make their way to wherever it was docked. But the *Kekada*?

The *Kekada* would come to them.

Within thirty seconds they heard a high-pitched whine trilling from the water. Under the waves, a light emanated, growing as it came up from the depths. The red ship broke the water about thirty yards off and kept coming, water streaming off as lights pulsed all along the black face, the dome of its head, and strobed up and down the length of its tapered edges, which looked almost like wings. As the bottom of the ship emerged, Gabriel heard mechanical groaning as the *Kekada* lurched, carried aloft by eight legs moving in time with one another.

Peter led the *Kekada* up the beach until it stood over them, as though they were in a grove of mechanical crab legs.

The iris below the ship glowed and opened, and Peter grabbed on, dragging himself up and inside, then Gabriel and Misty followed. Once they were inside the dive room, Gabriel opened the hatch into the bridge as the dive iris closed in the floor.

"Let's get off the beach before anyone notices us," Gabriel said. "We look like space aliens."

They slid into their chairs as the submarine loped back toward the water, the viewscreen image spinning. Waves crashed up and then they were under, fish darting aside as the legs retracted with a *clunk*, and they soared away into the surf.

"Take us out to a hundred-and-fifty-feet depth," Gabriel said. Peter said aye and the pumps in the walls rumbled as the *Kekada*'s hull began to fill, the engines shooting them forward and down.

"Where are we going?" Misty asked. Peter brought the sonar up to fill a quarter of the viewscreen. A yellow light sprang up on the sonar indicating the coordinates they had received. It was in the center of the inlet of the Bristol Channel that curved to meet the bay. "That is five miles off," he said.

"So it's close," Gabriel said. Now a second image in green appeared as the sonar hand swept around, indicating a ship. He looked back at Peter. "There they are. Can we hear them?"

Peter had his hand up to his ear, listening to one side of a pair of headphones. "Here we go." He tapped a button and the radio crackled to life with a man's voice, a low Scottish growl.

"*Sppskk* . . . SOS . . . Cargo Vessel *Tamerlaine*, we are taking on water. We are under attack from a . . . *skssk*."

Misty was typing and said, "*Tamerlaine*, yes, cargo ship, classification Neopanamax."

"*Neo*panamax?" Peter answered. He looked at the ceiling. This was a favorite game of his. "Okay, those are really big canal ships. So don't tell me, what is it, three hundred and sixty feet long?"

Misty snapped and pointed. "Three-sixty-six feet."

Peter held up his hands as though accepting the adulation of an imaginary crowd.

Gabriel gestured with his thumb toward the sonar screen. "But they say they're under *attack*."

"Yeah, from an *animal*," Peter said. "This is probably a hoax, Gabe. It's a joke. No animal is going to attack a ship that big."

"I'm not saying it's really an animal," Gabriel offered. "When the *Nautilus* first appeared people thought it was a narwhal. You heard that guy, he sounds like he's under attack from *something*. Can we answer him on his frequency?"

Peter tapped a few buttons and pointed to the intercom mics resting above the viewscreen. "Go."

Gabriel looked up and spoke to the mics. "Vessel *Tamerlaine*, this is Nemoship *Kekada*, we are en route to your position, say again attack from *what*?"

"We cannae tell!" the voice came back strong. The sound of waves splashing against hard surfaces drowned him out for a moment.

"How soon can we get there?" Gabriel asked Peter.

"Two minutes."

"What, say again?" Gabriel called.

The man's voice ratcheted out the words in an urgent, indecipherable bellow.

"What?" Gabriel slashed his hand across his throat and looked at Misty. "All I hear is yelling and splashing."

She made a bewildered face and shrugged, turning her palms up. *Got me.*

"Whoa," Peter said. Gabriel looked back at the viewscreen as Peter magnified the image. They could see the underside of the cargo vessel as the *Kekada* tilted upward, shooting toward it. But wrapped around the ship—not once but several times—was something that appeared to be an enormous cable.

As they grew closer, the image magnified further and now they could see the end of the thing, a bright tail that shone in the colorless underwater image. The end of the tail swished up and then deep into the water and back up again.

"I can't believe...," Gabriel whispered. "I've never heard of a snake that big in the ocean."

"Ocean's got a lotta secrets," Peter said.

"Fifty yards off slow," Gabriel said.

"SOS Cargo Vessel *Tamerlaine*...," came the man's voice.

"We'll arrive shortly!" Gabriel called.

The *Tamerlaine* jerked violently as the serpent moved it this way and that and tugged it down. An enormous burst of water sent bubbles everywhere around the cargo ship as a container fifty feet long dropped into the water and plummeted. At this rate the ship was liable to take on water and, considering the weight of the hundreds of cargo containers it was likely to be carrying, it would sink like a stone.

"Surface," Gabriel said. "I want to see the rest of it."

The *Kekada* broke the surface in seconds and Peter whipped them around to see the ship. As they rested on the surface, waves splashed in the lower part of the screen.

The cargo vessel's floodlights shone into the sky and cast beams of light all around the water, and Gabriel gasped.

Gnawing on the red-and-black prow of the cargo ship

was a snake's head that had to be twenty feet long. The head was triangular, like a python's. Massive white fangs punched holes into sections of the railing atop the ship, tearing chunks away and sending gear flying. Cables whipped through the air. The creature's eyes glistened wet and black. White stripes beginning at its nostrils flowed down its body, practically glowing.

"Holy mackerel." Peter got up, staring in awe. "That's a ... is that a *sea serpent?*" Peter said.

The creature's tail extended out beyond the ship, flopping wildly against the waves, and Peter maneuvered the *Kekada* back from it as best he could.

Gabriel closed his mouth. He remembered a time, shortly before he came to land, when one of the domes at Nemolab had cracked and water started coming in, threatening a garden that Gabriel had been in charge of. He'd run back and forth, while the water sprayed down, until his father told him: *Slow down. The world can spin out of control, but you don't have to.*

Next steps and next steps. "What we gotta do is get it off that ship."

Misty nodded. "Okay, Captain. Where do you wanna start?"

Just then the barbed, striped tail of the serpent whipped out of the water and into the air, high. When it began to whip down, Gabriel saw that the *Kekada* was in an unlucky spot.

"Brace," Gabriel said as he dropped into his chair.

At the word *brace*, emergency straps slammed over his shoulder and down to his hip with a *clack* that he heard echoed for Misty and Peter.

And then the tail hit the *Kekada* with a thunderous impact.

5

ALARM KLAXONS RANG throughout the bridge. The tail of the serpent smashed into the top of the submarine, pushing it twenty feet deeper into the water. As the tail slipped to the side of the ship, it tilted the *Kekada* far to port so that they were almost perfectly sideways. Then they seesawed back with nauseating force. Gabriel could barely keep his eyes open as he was thrown again against his restraints.

"Stabilizers!" he shouted. His stomach lurched as the ship twisted in the waves over and over again.

Peter shouted from his station, "Stabilizers coming back online."

The sound of powerful engines hummed all along the edges of the crab shell. Gabriel pushed himself back against his seat as the submarine righted, sliding back into regular alignment. "Dive! One hundred feet and fall back. We need to come up with a plan."

"Diving," Peter called, and they began to sink backward, putting distance between themselves and the serpent.

Gabriel rubbed his head. "Damage?"

"Minor," Misty said. "We dropped with the blow and the outer shell didn't have to absorb the whole impact. We, uh, have some leakage in the upper dome." She looked up. This was a small ship. The upper dome was right over their heads.

Gabriel ran through what he remembered of the upper dome. "That's the oxygen generators. If they short out, we'll have limited oxygen until we can fix it." He twisted in his seat. "What do you think—did it swat us on purpose?"

"You mean did the big snake deliberately strike us or just stumble over us? Does it matter?"

"I'm just trying to figure out if it's intelligent." Gabriel figured that if it was smart it would be a lot tougher to beat. Deadlier, in fact.

"No way of knowing yet," Misty said. "And nothing's changed, we still have to help the *Tamerlaine.*"

"Okay," Gabriel said. "Be on the lookout for the serpent's tail."

Peter scoffed. "Yeah, if it's all the same to you, I'm gonna be on the lookout for the whole dang thing."

"Options?" Gabriel called. On the screen, they were watching the serpent. More cargo containers splashed into the water, and the tail swished down, batting one container and sending it spinning off into the distance before it sank away.

"Pincer torpedoes," Misty said. Gabriel's Nemoships carried no conventional weapons, but they were outfitted with an array of tools and weapons that utilized a Nemotech called pincer energy. "We aim pincer torpedoes at the serpent..."

"And hope we don't hit the ship?" Gabriel asked. "If we miss the snake and hit the *Tamerlaine*, we could wind up hitting a barrel of oil and blowing the ship up." It was a focused energy that could do a lot of damage but that by design was less likely to be deadly when the user didn't want such an outcome. Gabriel never did. But only *less* likely. Not impossible. No weapon was truly safe.

"You can't aim for the head when it's silhouetted against the sky?" Peter asked. "That way if you miss, the torpedo just goes past."

"I love that you think I can do that." Misty put one hand on her hip and swept the other across her station. "We got all kinds of crazy stuff, but smart missiles are not among them," Misty said. "I can aim. But once the torpedo comes up out of the water, it'll start going wild in the air. Torpedoes aren't meant to fly through the air. Plus *aiming* isn't a cakewalk, either; look how much the snake is moving around."

Peter waved his hands. "Okay, then...not torpedoes. We use the *Kekada*'s legs and try to grab it by the jaw."

"Grab its jaw?" Gabriel asked.

"You know, like...Tarzan with an alligator."

"What's a *Tarzan*?" Gabriel asked.

Misty stared. "Really?"

"It doesn't matter," Peter said with a sigh. "We can grab the jaw."

Gabriel shook his head. He pictured it all. "Okay... let's say we do that. We pull the snake down until its head is in the water, then somehow grab its jaw with the *Kekada*'s legs. The snake will start to whip us around. We don't have suspension and stabilizers enough in the body of the *Kekada* to keep us from flipping over and over again. Probably it'll drag us right out of the water and shake us. And I don't care how good these straps are, it'll knock us right out."

"Up periscope," Misty said, tapping buttons to execute her own command. The viewscreen split and they watched as a camera loosed itself from the edge of the *Kekada* and shot up through the water. The *Kekada*'s periscope was a floating camera mounted on a long cable. It splashed out and landed on the pounding waves, and they saw again the serpent with its massive teeth. "You know...this serpent isn't natural," she muttered. "We could go out with Katanas and pincer rifles."

Gabriel thought. Katanas were small, one-person craft that he and Misty used for zipping around when a big ship wouldn't do. They were like motorcycles, you just got on and *went.* "The snake is big and clumsy. We could probably move around it and it would be hard to hit us. But if it *did* hit us…"

"We just dive." Misty shrugged. "Move and dive and move and dive. And when we're up, we start laying on the snake with the pincer rifles."

Gabriel nodded, unclicking his safety belt. "Yeah."

Misty unfastened and they began walking to the door to the dive room.

"Wait, what, you're doing *what*?" Peter asked.

"We can get a good bead on it from the surface with pincer rifles." Gabriel talked to him from inside the dive room, holding the door as Misty went around him. "Don't worry, if it's gonna attack anything it's more likely to be you."

"Great." Peter shook his head. "I'd tell you to be careful, but you guys are nuts anyway, so it doesn't matter."

"Noted." Gabriel looked around at the inside of the dive room. It was a mess—after the pounding the snake had given the ship, cables and equipment lay strewn across the floor. Misty hit the flood lever and they had to sift through a mess of tow cables to find their masks. By then the water was at their knees.

"We gotta do a better job of securing stuff." Misty went to the lockers and grabbed a pair of rifles, tossing one to Gabriel.

"We'll design some wall fasteners. Peter," Gabriel said

into his mouthpiece as the water came to his neck, "we're headed out to meet the snake."

"Copy. Listen, if your rifles don't have enough effect, don't hang around out there. I'll fire a torpedo somewhere on the other side of the snake just to make a ruckus and you guys hurry on back," Peter answered in his earpiece. "Then we'll try something else."

The water reached the ceiling and Gabriel and Misty dropped through the dive iris into the ocean. The water was frigid against his neck and face, but the warming gels in the suit worked to counteract the effect. They moved along the underside until they reached a pair of long, red, bulbous housings on the underside of the crab ship. The housings were set to respond to their gloves and they each unlocked one.

As the red bulbs retracted, Gabriel and Misty immediately set to unlatching the Katanas. Gabriel touched the ignition on his as it dropped, and the vehicle throbbed to life. Next to him, Misty straddled her Katana and dropped, disappearing into the depths before zipping back up beside him. They dove under the nose of the *Kekada* and away from the crab ship. After they had traveled a good thirty yards, Gabriel pointed up and they headed for the surface.

All sound had gone away now except the dull thrumming of the engines in the water, and their own chatter in Gabriel's ear. And his breathing. The sound of his own breath while diving was so constant, he didn't even hear it anymore unless he focused, usually to remind himself to breathe slowly.

~~~

The moment Gabriel and Misty broke the surface, the sounds of the ship and the snake nearly overwhelmed him. He heard smashing and saw bursts of flame as engines and machinery on the ship exploded. The snake continued to gnaw.

"All right," Misty said. "It's time we got its attention. I'll try for its eyes. You try to hit its mouth."

"Right," Gabriel said. He racked the pincer rifle and aimed in the general direction of the serpent's head. With the Katana bucking under him like it was, aiming was practically impossible.

Firing the pincer rifle was like using a firehose. Even under the best of circumstances, you had to rely on dragging the arc of energy where you wanted it to go. Aiming was even harder when riding on choppy waves.

Gabriel fired, the rifle dancing against his arm, and a long arc of energy buzzed toward the snake, impacting and sparking against the ship's hull. He dragged the rifle sideways, sending the undulating arc of pincer energy right into the creature's jaws.

Misty dragged her own arc to the side until she managed to hit the serpent's left eye, and the creature howled.

The great serpent swiveled its head, trying to avoid the

arc, and for a moment whipped its head back, baring its neck. Gabriel saw something that nearly made him drop his rifle.

Right below the creature's jaw on the underside of its head was something he could only think of as a metal basket.

The basket looked to be about the size of his Katana, and it was made of a silver metal, with a strobing light on the top end that flickered on and off.

"What is *that?*" he yelled as they kept firing. He gestured to follow and whisked the Katana forward, zipping closer to the serpent.

"Not natural," Misty said. "Blinky boxes don't grow on snakes. You know what, shoot the blinky box."

They laid on with the pincers, the arcs dancing as they tried to aim under the snake's jaw. Gabriel managed to glance his arc of energy against the box but only briefly, the metal sparking as he did. But always the snake dodged and he had to re-aim, missing again and again.

"Guys!" Peter shouted in his ear. "You've got company coming in fast... Small craft, sixty knots, on your six."

Small craft?

Gabriel turned, looking at the choppy waves.

Misty shouted in his headset, "Gabriel, dive, it's striking!"

He didn't look. Gabriel throttled the Katana and dove, shooting under the waves to see the faint sidelights of Misty's Katana. She turned to starboard and he to port, and for a moment he took the opportunity to look back to see the snake's nose dip into the water and yank back up.

"Back up," Gabriel said. "Hit it again."

They both erupted from the water into the night once more. The snake was rearing back its head to strike.

Misty fired, aiming at its face, and the creature writhed and snapped again, great fangs bared. Gabriel aimed at its eyes, and it reared its head, so he tried again for the box.

Over his shoulder a bubbling, alien sound, ratcheting like a machine, rose. Gabriel and Misty both paused, looking in the direction of the strange, repeating wail: *whee-oooo-pop-pop-pop.*

A craft emerged from the water.

It was small, barely big enough for a single pilot, and speckled exactly the color and shine of an electric blue ram fish on all sides except for its glass canopy. The strange blue craft swept toward the serpent, its call louder now. *Whee-oooo-pop-pop-pop.*

Inside the glass canopy Gabriel saw a girl with dark brown skin and blue goggles. Her chin brushed against a frilled collar that ended at a pair of gold epaulettes at her shoulders.

Two words echoed through Gabriel's head: *It's you.*

As the strange call repeated, the snake swayed as if stunned.

"Now's our chance," Misty said, firing again.

"Please!" A voice came from the little ship. Gabriel could see her crying out from inside the cockpit. "Please. Let me handle him."

Misty called, "Don't stop now, it's loosening its grip on the ship."

"Please," the girl responded. "It's my responsibility."

Gabriel looked at Misty as the speckled craft kept calling with its weird whistles and pops. The snake, mesmerized, uncoiled, pulling away. As it let the big ship go it drifted into the water, ignoring Gabriel and Misty and following the ululations of the blue craft.

And as suddenly as it had appeared, the blue craft whipped around and dove, still whistling, and the snake dove after it. On the cargo ship, men were scurrying over the deck, putting out fires. The railings were twisted beyond repair, but the ship was still afloat. They would have to put into port.

Floating in the wake of the disappeared serpent, Gabriel and Misty looked at each other, the flames and lights from the ship illuminating their confused faces.

Misty pursed her lips. *Whaaat?*

"Oh, we gotta..." He whipped his hand, pointing down. "Totally."

They dove instantly, throttling their Katanas together and swooping down as fast as they could go.

They rode in the direction the snake had gone as

Gabriel called back to the *Kekada*. "Peter, call the authorities to help the ship."

Gabriel caught a glimmer of light up ahead, the speckled craft, and saw the whipping tail of the serpent following it.

Through the water he could still hear the whistles and pops. "Peter," he called, "I see them. How's the ship?"

"Coast guard is on the way," Peter said. "They've got water coming in, but they'll last a few hours."

Ahead of Gabriel and Misty, the snake had finally caught up to the speckled ship and was now right on it. It snapped at the craft and for a moment Gabriel thought that the serpent would crunch it in its jaws.

The girl inside the cockpit looked back, and just then the snake lunged and grabbed hold of the ship, crunching through the hull and sending speckled bits flying in the water. The canopy popped open and the girl swam out as the whistle and pops sputtered and died. The snake shook the craft in its mouth.

The girl had two short staffs in her arms. She clicked them together and they erupted as flares.

"Shoot it," Gabriel said, and he and Misty flew in the Katanas down and under the snake, shooting again, the arcs of pincer energy laying into the creature's neck and aiming at the box. As the pincer energy laid into the box, the metal began to smoke and curl, until finally it tore open in a brief spout of flame.

The snake reared back as if dazed and shook its head. Misty and Gabriel began shooting again. It coiled back in the water, and finally turned and fled downward and away.

Gabriel looked at the girl and saw that in fact she was just about his and Misty's age. Where had she come from? Was she one of the secret visitors that he had been looking for?

The girl twisted the staffs in her hands, and he saw that they were able to propel her in the water as she pushed herself back away from them. Gabriel waved his arms and pointed toward the surface.

The girl hesitated. Then she nodded and they all headed up.

When he and Misty broke through the surface, Gabriel could see the ship, miles away, smoke still pouring and visible against the sky.

The girl popped up next. The waves were loud as the Katanas floated while the girl treaded water. Her strange Elizabethan collar seemed to pull upward against her shoulders, giving her buoyancy in the waves.

They were frozen for a moment. *You're the one we've been looking for*, he thought. He wanted to laugh out loud. He had a thousand questions, starting with *My buddy thinks you're Maelstrom*. But for now, she was far out in the ocean alone.

"You can't stay out here," Gabriel called over the noisy waves. "We have a ship. Would you like to come back to it?"

The girl looked around. She nodded in the direction the snake had gone. "I really, really wish you hadn't done that."

"The ship was in trouble," he said. "And I'm not sure, but I think we've been looking for you."

The girl shook her head angrily. "I don't know where it will *go* now. I don't know how it will get by."

Misty didn't respond to that, but said, "You can't just stay out here on the water. Do you want to come with us?"

Gabriel called into his mic, "Peter?"

"I'm here."

"Come up close to the surface. We're bringing some-one with us."

Shortly, Gabriel felt the waves swell as the *Kekada* rose underneath them. "Follow us," he said.

"You're him, aren't you?" The girl was staring at him, and then she broke eye contact to regard Misty. "And you. Both of you, you're the *Obscure*."

Misty and Gabriel exchanged bewildered glances. She knew about the *Obscure*! "We have to talk," Gabriel answered. "Dive with us. We'll go into our ship through a dive iris in the bottom."

They dove in the Katanas and he looked back and saw that the girl was diving, too, propelled by the staffs in her hands. They swept down and under, and she hung back as Gabriel and Misty secured the Katanas underneath the burnished red hull.

Gabriel opened the iris and Misty swam up first. When

Gabriel was up, he looked down to where the girl hung in the water, looking up. He waved again, *Come on*.

She swam up and Misty closed the iris behind them. They floated in the water as it drained away.

And then there they were, the crew and the stranger who Gabriel couldn't believe he had actually found. She looked sad and defeated, and worst of all, trapped.

"You're safe," he said, seeing the fear in her eyes. "The moment you want to leave, say so. I'm Gabriel. Gabriel Nemo."

"Nemo," she whispered. "So it's true. And you?"

"Misty."

The girl lifted her goggles above her braided black hair. "I'm Cora Land. I come from Dinas Nautilus."

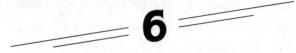

6

WHEN GABRIEL OPENED the door to the bridge, the girl called Cora froze for a moment. Misty ushered her in, and Gabriel followed. She stood there at the back of the small bridge with her mouth hanging open, and slowly spun.

Peter got out of his chair. "Uh...hello." Peter looked to the other two—should this stranger be allowed on the bridge? But Gabriel had already made that call.

"That's Peter," Gabriel said. "Helm. Peter, this is Cora."

"It's..." Cora extended her arms.

Gabriel moved slowly to the side and watched the strange girl take in the whole bridge, the ribs running up the walls and the knobs of the shelves, the leather of the seats.

She wrung her hands. "It's. So. *Nemo*."

Misty pushed her hair back and snorted. "Oh, you should have seen the *Obscure*."

"Right," Cora responded, almost to herself. She went to the shelf that ran under the viewscreen, touching the small computer screens and various knobs and keypads. "Right, this isn't the *Obscure*."

"I'm still not clear on ... How do you know about the *Obscure*?" Gabriel asked.

"Everyone knows about you," Cora said. "Everyone who's interested in the outside."

"Everyone where?" Gabriel asked. "You said you're from somewhere called Dinas. Dinas Nautilus."

"Yes," Cora said, crouching beside Peter's station to peer up at the wiring underneath. "The City."

"It's a city?"

"*Dinas* means *city*." Her hand found a panel underneath Peter's station and she opened it, then stuck her hand up into the underside. She got on her back and put her face up against the open panel. "Fascinating. What is this wiring insulation? It's not rubber."

"It's a seaweed-based polymer," Peter said. "But I'm not sure you should be sticking your hand up in there."

"Will something shock me?" she asked, swinging her head out to look at Peter.

"If you pull something loose."

"Why would I do that?"

"At this point I got no idea." Peter shrugged. "I actually thought you were with Maelstrom."

Cora grimaced. So she knew about Maelstrom.

Gabriel watched as she studied the wiring of the *Kekada*. "*Dinas* means *city*? In what language?"

Cora crawled out and rose, pointing to the other station and asking Misty, "Is that one yours?"

"Yes."

She came around it. "What is it, ops?"

"Yep."

"Fantastic." Cora laughed. Then she added, "Welsh. *Dinas* is *city* in Welsh."

"So you speak Welsh?" Gabriel asked. "Does the City of Nautilus speak Welsh?" It was the first time he'd put the sentence together, and it made his whole body shiver. The City of Nautilus was a place, and this girl was from there. His mind reeled. It wasn't just a little craft or two. There was a *city*. Maybe an undersea dome like Nemolab.

"Sometimes," she said.

A light flashed and Peter called out, "Hang on. We got another ship, closing fast."

"What ship?" Gabriel asked. On the sonar screen, a large submarine was coming up from below.

Cora looked up at the sonar and sighed. "Yeah. Probably the *O'Connell*."

"The *O'Connell*?" Peter asked.

"The *Daniel O'Connell*," she said.

Gabriel said to Misty, "Daniel O'Connell was an Irish politician; he was a hero of Captain Nemo's. There was a portrait of him in the gallery of the *Nautilus*."

"The things you know," Peter said.

On the viewscreen, a rounded shape rose. It was a submarine all right—but milky white, long and bulbous, with shimmering lights running down its sides. Gabriel saw no familiar textures. It didn't look like metal at all. Through the water it looked like rubber or sharkskin, even, but it measured as wide as the *Kekada* and twice as long. Almost the size of the *Obscure*—not what he would call a big submarine, but big enough. He saw no ports or torpedo shafts. It was as though a great glowing mollusk had emerged from the depths and hung in the water just about a hundred yards away.

"I can barely see any heat," Peter said. "It's camouflaged pretty well. This is your ship?"

"Not my ship," she said. "But they're— It's our ship."

"Can you contact them?" Gabriel asked.

"They're contacting me," she said. She took off her goggles and laid them on the shelf that ran around the inside of the bridge.

"This is Cora."

A male voice rose from the speakers in the goggles. "Cora? Are you all right?"

"I'm fine," she said. "I was pursuing Kaa."

"Kaa is the snake?" Gabriel asked.

"Who are you with?" the voice came back.

Gabriel spoke up. "This is Gabriel Nemo of the Nemo-ship *Kekada*."

There was a pause. "Nemoship?"

"They rescued me," the girl said. "Kaa was out of control. He's only gotten more erratic since he escaped."

Gabriel tried to take this in. So this girl's people had been holding the creature. The control box obviously had been put there by someone.

"This is an unauthorized...," the voice began.

"Come on, Nils," Cora said. "We can't just lose a snake and expect it to be okay."

"Who am I speaking to?" Gabriel asked.

"This is Nils Ramoray," the man said. "And I urge you not to detain that girl."

Cora whispered, "He's really protective."

"Cora, you need to come back."

"Nils, did you hear what he said? It's a Nemoship!"

Nils sighed. "Don't you understand you're breaking *every rule*? I need you to swim across."

"Don't you think that Minerva will want to meet them?" Cora said. Another name Gabriel hadn't heard.

"It's not the time," Nils said. "Now if you're being held captive, I want them to know that they will be *boarded*."

"I'm not being held captive," Cora said. "Nils, this isn't

some drylander ship. Just think what Minerva would say if she knew we met the Nemos and we did nothing."

"Sir?" Gabriel called. He paused. He was talking to these strangers for the first time. What could convey the feelings he had without sounding...strange? "Captain Ramoray. I want you to know that I've been...looking for you. We've come so far. All the way across the world. And it would mean the world to us to see your home. We keep secrets. We'll keep yours. Just please...let us see it."

"I'm afraid that's out of the question."

"You know what they're capable of," Cora said. "We can learn so much from them."

"Gabriel," Misty whispered. "Have you thought about this?"

Nils paused for a long time. Finally he said, "We will send you the coordinates."

"All right," Gabriel said. "Give me a moment with my crew."

He gestured Misty and Peter into the dive room. He left the door open and looked back at Cora, holding up a hand, *wait*. Then he said, "Okay, talk to me."

"They don't seem like Maelstrom, that's for sure," Misty said. They kept their voices low.

"Sure," Peter agreed. "So it seems like they're not Maelstrom. They're smarter than Maelstrom, which ain't better. They did apparently make a big snake, or just had one somehow, and they sicced it on that cargo ship."

"Cora said it got loose," Gabriel said.

"And who's Cora, again?" Peter said. "We don't know if that's true."

"Yeah, but she didn't say it to us, she said it to *him*, to this Captain Ramoray." Gabriel was bouncing in his shoes. "We've been looking for these guys. So, what are the risks if we follow them?"

"Well, Gabriel, the *risk* is you're following a bunch of *strangers* somewhere that *they* know, and *you* don't. I mean, that's like general-purpose risky."

Gabriel sighed. "We have the *Kekada*. We can defend ourselves."

"Yeah?" Peter asked. "Okay, so what if they lead us over a ridge into an ambush of ten of those weird milk subs waiting for us. Suppose those ten have EMP devices and knock us out. Heck, suppose they just have torpedoes. How many torpedoes do you think we can dodge? How about this: How many torpedo *hits* do you think we can *take*?"

"I get it." Gabriel nodded. They had twenty countermeasures, small cylinders they could shoot out to intercept torpedoes, but when they ran out, they would be left to just try to avoid being hit. And the *Kekada* was not a very big sub. Two rooms plus the lower compartment, the modular engines and pumps, and other equipment. Plus, the oxygen systems were above. That was it. *Nothing* could afford a hit.

Up on the screen, the white sub waited in silence. Cora had leaned on the shelf with her arms folded.

"They're not gonna fire on us with her aboard," Gabriel said.

"We should send a note back to our parents." Misty pulled out her phone.

"Yeah," Peter said. "When they wake up, they're gonna love, *Hey, some bad guys threw a big snake at a cargo ship, so we thought we'd accept their invitation back to their place.* Maybe these guys'll have Tofurkey, too."

"Okay, you know," Gabriel said as he looked out onto the bridge at the golden pin with the message on it, "*I'm* absolutely inclined to follow. But we haven't been kidnapped."

"Not yet."

"My point is, they haven't tried to take the ship. We still have it. As of right now we're free, so we have some choices. Look, I *have* to go. But if you guys…"

"Oh, this again," Peter moaned. "Adventure awaits, and answer it I must, but you two are welcome to go back to school."

Gabriel scoffed. "You just listed all the bad stuff that could happen…"

"That's *what I'm here for*!" Peter wrung his hands. "When are you gonna stop giving us this speech?"

"I mean, I don't know, six years at least."

"Misty?" Peter turned to her, grabbing a peach out of the cooler he flipped open. He took a bite. "Have you heard the speech?"

"Yep." She nodded. "I heard the speech."

"Okay, and are we past the speech or is the *Kekada* gonna drop you and me off on the beach?"

"I already got my suit wet," Misty said. "So no, we're in this."

"There ya go," Peter said, talking through a mouthful of peach as he gestured with the fruit at Gabriel. "I'm just saying, we're *with* you. But look. We gotta be careful."

Gabriel nodded. Peter was right. "So . . . let's do that, let's be careful. Misty, whatever the coordinates are, as soon as we get them, send them to the *Nebula*. I want my sister to know where we're going."

"Totally," she said. "Yeah." Misty clearly thought it was a good idea, but she also kind of idolized Gabriel's sister. If there were a Nerissa Nemo action figure, Gabriel suspected Misty would have that on her station instead of the Troll doll.

"I like that, too," Peter said. "It's a little less nuts."

Gabriel breathed and nodded, and they walked back onto the bridge. He turned to Cora and spoke up. "Okay. We'd be happy to receive the coordinates."

A light plinked on Peter's console and he threw the coordinates up on the screen. A little green light shone about sixty miles west of the mouth of the Bristol Channel in the Celtic Sea.

"That's about two hundred miles from here," Peter said. "About a hundred miles from the southern tip of Ireland."

Was it possible that the crew of the *Nautilus* had come to Wales, and settled in a city near Ireland in the Celtic Sea? They hadn't done much looking there. And why the activity around Wales now?

Gabriel turned to Peter. "Follow them at whatever speed they go."

"Assuming they can do seventy knots, figure it'll be three hours," Misty said.

"We'll follow you," Gabriel said toward Cora's goggles. "Our helmsman will be in touch with yours in case you need to communicate."

"Very well," came back Nils. "Then we shall embark immediately."

Outside, the milky-white sub began to move, rolling toward them in the water and dipping down. It disappeared for a moment and then came around and into view again and began moving off. Peter began moving, keeping a distance of about a quarter mile.

"They're moving, forty-five knots," Peter said.

"Okay," Gabriel answered, dropping back into his chair. "Match their speed and maintain this distance."

The *O'Connell* picked up speed. Peter slammed the throttle forward and the *Kekada* began to soar through the water.

"Here we go," Gabriel said.

Misty fired off the coordinates as the *Kekada* shot through the water after the *O'Connell*.

7

THE OCEAN FLOWED about them in murky green that speckled with life. Gabriel could be mesmerized by the view of the sea, but this time, as they followed the *O'Connell*, he was more interested in their strange visitor.

Cora continued to roam the bridge, peering into panels. Her wandering seemed to make Peter especially nervous, because he followed her with his eyes. Finally he reached down to a cooler unit below his chair. He opened it and brought out a fruit and held it out. "Peach?"

"Thank you," she said, and took it. She nibbled it without hesitation, Gabriel noticed. And without any sense of curiosity or strangeness. So her City of Nautilus had fresh fruit.

"So is your city a dome?" Peter asked Cora. "Nemolab

is a dome. What else are you going to put at the bottom of the ocean?"

Cora laughed. "It's not a dome. It's a city. What's Nemolab?" Gabriel described to the girl the domed complex where he'd grown up.

Cora seemed fascinated. She turned to Misty and Peter. "But *you* didn't grow up there?"

Misty shook her head, laughing. "No, we're from California."

"Drylanders," Cora said. There was a certain wistfulness to it. "Oh, tell me what it's like."

Peter kept the *O'Connell* displayed on the viewscreen as he made other camera views flit across the top and bottom of the screen. "Tell you what *what's* like? California?"

"I just…" Cora chewed on the peach and said, "I just… I always wanted to know what that world is like. To have the sun on your shoulders every day."

"Uh, well," Misty said, "there's a lot of that."

"What do you do every day?" Cora asked. "Do you live in…they're called houses? Right? I've read books. Do you go to school?"

"Yeah," Peter said. "But actually now we go to school on the ocean. Before that I lived with my mom in an apartment."

"What's that like?" Cora asked. "How do you, you know, get around? I've seen pictures. Of…automobiles?"

"Huh. You've really never been on land before," Peter said.

"It's against the rules," Cora said. "We're never supposed to be seen by the drylanders."

Peter looked at Gabriel. "That sounds familiar. What is it with you sea people and the crazy secrecy?" He looked back at Cora. "When Gabriel first got to land, everything he knew about the world he learned from watching *Purple Rain.*"

When Cora wrinkled her brow in confusion Misty rapidly shot through a catalog of concepts: "That's a movie. An old one. And a movie is..."

"We have those," Cora said, "though I've never seen a drylander film."

"You have your own *movies?*" Peter asked.

Gabriel was thinking of his own time at Nemolab, which was mostly dedicated to schooling, research, and occasional movie nights watching stuff brought in from above, including *Purple Rain*, a movie about a young musician somewhere in the middle of the United States.

But as fascinating as it would be to find out what kind of movies an undersea city made to show to itself, there were more important things he wanted to understand. Gabriel leaned forward in his captain's chair, his elbows on his knees. "All these rescues you've been doing. Is that just you?"

Cora held up both hands. "Please don't mention it. They don't know. Like I said..."

"Against the rules." Gabriel nodded. "Okay. We won't mention it."

~~~

After an hour of traveling they pushed downward, now at seven hundred feet. The closed Nemo ship-to-ship communicator lit up and chirped, and a familiar voice rang out from the speakers over the viewscreen. "You're going where?" It was Nerissa Nemo, Gabriel's sister.

Gabriel's heart swelled as he heard her voice. He had no idea where Nerissa was right now. She was an outlaw, wanted by half the navies on the planet for her penchant for sabotaging ships she deemed dangerous to sea life. She made sure not to injure people, but she was generally regarded as dangerous, a terrorist even. Nerissa was the closest to the legacy of Captain Nemo that there ever had been.

"Hey, Nerissa!" Misty chirped. She didn't wave, but her voice sounded like she was anyway.

"Misty, what's he got you doing?" Nerissa said.

"We're going about a hundred miles off the southern tip of Ireland," Gabriel said. "We encountered a strange sub..."

"A very strange sub," Peter shouted.

"And they've, uh, invited us to their...their base, I guess."

"Do Misty's and Peter's parents know where you are?" Nerissa asked. She sounded like she was scowling.

"Who's this?" Cora asked.

"That's Gabriel's sister, Nerissa," Peter said. "And this is the part I love: The girl's wanted for international terrorism but she's surprisingly stiff on keeping parents in the loop."

"I just don't want anybody's folks calling the police," Nerissa said. "So, how do you know they're not Maelstrom?"

"Wait, Nerissa *Nemo*?" Cora exclaimed. "I've heard of her!"

"You have someone aboard?"

"She's a citizen of this... Dinas Nautilus. The City of Nautilus." Gabriel caught her up. He left out the giant snake. "They're really the descendants of the *Nautilus*."

"Wow," Nerissa finally whispered. She sounded impressed. Gabriel didn't blame her. If somehow these people really *were* connected to the *Nautilus* crew, that would be amazing. "Okay. I'm sending you a message."

She signed off and after a moment his wristband chirped. Something she wanted him to read without anyone else hearing.

Record what you can. And don't let them
corner you. If they're really who you hope
they are—and Gabriel, I use the word hope

deliberately—don't be dazzled. They've kept themselves hidden. We don't know why.

"Gabriel, we're approaching the Porcupine Seabight," Peter said.

They were flying along about one hundred feet off the silty bottom known as the Celtic Shelf, and Gabriel saw ahead of them, beyond the *O'Connell*, a cliff, and darkness beyond.

The *O'Connell* disappeared over the side and the *Kekada* rushed behind it.

"Slow to sixty knots," Gabriel said.

The ocean floor sloped suddenly and dramatically as both ships tilted. The *O'Connell* visibly slowed, and Peter matched its speed, following the strange vessel down along the slope.

"Would you get a load of this?" Peter said. "It's like the Grand Canyon down here."

"I've read about the Grand Canyon," Cora offered. "Have you seen it?"

"Once," Peter said. "Kind of required."

"Totally," Misty added.

"I've seen some of California and about three miles of Wales," Gabriel said. "Maybe it's time."

Below them they saw underwater mountain ranges towering with sediment and disappearing far away into darkness. They dropped into a canyon, and Peter kept the *Kekada* 150 feet from the right edge, close enough that Gabriel could see glimmering, glowing sea life flickering along the walls.

Misty was reading. "This whole deep-water basin is made up of rifts that split open two hundred and fifty-two million years ago. It's huge, and deep, and yes, there are a lot of places to hide."

"Are these international waters?" Gabriel asked.

"Nope, technically we are in Ireland," she said.

They had lost the *O'Connell* in the canyon, but Gabriel saw a pink glow emanating around the corner. It pulsed as it glowed, lighting up the rocks and reflecting off tiny shellfish and crabs that clung to the rocks.

"Slow," Gabriel said. Where were they going? "Let's see what we've got."

He held his breath despite himself as they rounded the rocky curve and the *Kekada* leveled off and suddenly, light was everywhere.

In a sweeping valley at the bottom of the ridge that had to measure seven miles to the next mountain, Gabriel beheld more of the long, pulsing pink lights on the floor, laying out their path.

Up ahead, they saw the source of the greatest pulsing light: A great tower rose seventy feet from the ocean floor, its lamp rotating in a lighthouse on top, sided with—or at least the material seemed to be—brass and silver. The tower and lighthouse sat atop a large square building of the same colors. At each corner, enormous carvings of heads and shoulders reflected pink light.

"Oh, they're figureheads," Misty said. "Like you'd find at the front of a ship."

Peter magnified the image of the figurehead nearest them and Gabriel saw that it was far too large to be the actual figurehead of any ship he had ever seen. He couldn't tell what it was carved from—possibly marble, possibly coral, but swirling with pink. It was a woman in a Greek helmet. At the next corner was another female figurehead, this one wearing a French admiral's helmet. The other two they couldn't see clearly, but each wore a head cover of some kind, and each was the length of the kind of ship they seemed to suggest.

"They're like ship's prows on a compass," Misty said. She sounded amazed. "I mean, the *tower* is like a compass, and each corner has a figurehead." The compass tower sat on yet another enormous building nearly three times larger, and long, the shape of a ship's deck. All told, this lower building-shaped-like-a-ship had to be eleven hundred feet long.

"Great googly-moogly, it's enormous," Peter whispered.

"Well," Cora said. "It *has* to be."

The crew glanced at one another. Gabriel could see a palpable nervousness, but they weren't about to let that interfere with their exploration. It made him feel more indebted to them, beholden to them for their trust.

Peter pushed the *Kekada* down, down to nine hundred feet, as they dropped slowly behind the *O'Connell*, eventually coming to rest on shadowy spots on the roof of the building, not far from the walls of the compass tower.

"I don't see where they hook up," Peter said. At Nemolab, as all the crew had experienced, umbilical tubes hooked to the underside of the Nemoships, allowing the crew to move down and into the building. But here—

Suddenly the whole square that the *O'Connell* sat upon shook loose, seams appearing in the silt. The square began to lower, carrying the *O'Connell* down and out of view.

The lights Peter was following stopped at another shadowy area in the silt, and he looked at Gabriel. "Gabriel?"

Don't let them corner you, Nerissa had said. But Nerissa was all wrong. They weren't cornered. They were invited.

"That's an elevator," Cora explained as she nodded at the shadowy place to set down. "The way in."

Peter nodded. The *Kekada* moved and settled over the square. "Okay ... I'm dropping the legs." Gabriel heard machinery moving below them, and the ship settled on its eight legs.

Then the platform began to move, and Gabriel watched as the viewscreen showed a thick hide of metal, coral, and wood slide past them. They were lowering into darkness and all was black for half a second.

"Oh boy," Peter said.

And then they were lowering into a hangar. Gabriel stared at the viewscreen as they dropped into a vast room wide enough that the *O'Connell* sat fifty feet away, submerged in the flooded hangar just as they were. Beyond that, he saw other large ships, some of milk-white design, some with the colorful scales of the ship that Cora had piloted.

The flooded hangar was dark, lit up mainly by yellow lights along the walls, and one main window up ahead, through which Gabriel could see several people working in some kind of control room. All wore dark tunics, one with a frilly collar similar to Cora's. As this man talked to the other two, Gabriel heard a heavy clanging sound from up above.

"It's like a giant dive room," Misty said. And then Gabriel knew that the sound he had heard must have been a sliding door closing the opening that they had lowered through. The hangar rumbled, and at once the water began to rush out somehow, the machinery in the hangar growing louder and harsher as the water swept away. The water drizzled off the *Kekada* until they were looking through the viewscreen at the puddled floor, and a pair of double doors near the control room slid open.

"Gabriel, look at that," Misty said, pointing. In the back of the hangar, a great double door closed, bringing together an enormous crest that said:

MIM
DINAS NAUTILUS

8

AS SOON AS the water had receded, Gabriel saw three people, two men and a woman, coming down a ramp as it lowered from the *O'Connell*. In front was a tall man with curly brown hair and a strong jaw, and skin that was somewhere between Cora's and Gabriel's, wearing a frilly collar and goggles similar to the ones that Cora wore. He stood for a moment in front of the *O'Connell* and held up a hand toward the cameras in the face of the *Kekada*.

"That's Nils," Cora said.

Gabriel looked to his crew and said, "Well, I guess it's time to meet the locals."

Cora joined the crew as they headed into the dive room. Misty knelt and opened the iris. Gabriel was the first out, dropping down to the hangar below. He felt the slickness of the metal tiles and called, "Careful, it's slippery," as Cora, Misty, and Peter dropped down and stood once more surrounded by the legs of the crab.

Cora ran past him and jumped into Nils's arms. "We found them."

Nils laughed. "I see that you did." He turned and very slowly stretched out his hand.

Gabriel received the very firm handshake but couldn't keep himself from looking around at the enormous hangar. "I'm Gabriel Nemo. This is Misty, who is in charge of operations, and Peter, our helmsman."

"Nils Ramoray," he said. "Commander of the Watch. What did you call this ship?" Nils asked, walking over to run his hand along the black face of the Nemoship.

"*Kekada*," Gabriel said. "It means—"

"*Crab*," Nils said. He turned back. He tilted his head in a conciliatory way. "Of course. Welcome to Dinas Nautilus. I want to thank you for saving Cora. She's sort of a... favorite of the pilots of the Watch. A fantastic pilot herself. We need her."

Cora blushed slightly.

Nils regarded the crew thoughtfully, his hand to his chin. "As much as I wish I could ask you a million questions... I need to introduce you to the director."

Gabriel nodded. "Okay. Absolutely."

"If you'll follow me," Nils said. They began walking

toward the control room with the large windows. Next to a staircase that led up to the control room was an enormous pair of double doors, clearly the entrance to the hangar. As Nils neared, the double doors slammed open.

Gabriel felt a rush of exhilaration. Beyond the doors spread a wide balcony that shone with different colors, swirling with cherrylike wood and pink coral. And beyond that: trees.

Nils led them out onto the balcony—Gabriel noticed that every railing was studded with little cameo sculptures of faces, probably people from the City—and down into a great room.

No, he thought, *not a room, more like a park*, several stories deep and high. Gabriel couldn't see the end of it. Here and there, people in outfits similar to those worn by Cora and Nils picked fruit from trees and gathered their harvest in woven green baskets.

They began to follow a beige walkway next to well-manicured grass.

"What *is* this?" Peter asked in astonishment. "I feel like I'm in a park."

"I was thinking the exact same thing," Gabriel said. He looked up. Far above them, what appeared to be clouds hung in a field of powder blue.

Gabriel looked at Cora. "The ceiling looks like the sky?"

Cora nodded. "It turns dark blue at night. With stars."

Gabriel laughed with delight and looked at Misty. "We *never* thought of that."

"Who?" Nils asked, looking back.

"Nemolab," Gabriel said.

Out of nowhere a small creature sprang at Nils. Gabriel caught a flash of light green as the creature bounced on small muscular legs up onto Nils's head. It used a long green tail to take Nils's goggles and then throw them into the grass as it leapt back down to the walkway.

"Holy mackerel," Peter said.

The creature in front of them appeared to be something like a monkey—it was just two feet tall, but its color was green, its body was covered in scales, and on its wide face were gills.

Nils sighed. "Why is Ricou out?"

"Looks like one of your mother's experiments got away," Cora said. "You *know* that if Minerva catches him running around, she won't be happy."

This was the third time Gabriel had heard the name *Minerva* used in something like a warning.

Nils muttered to himself and then whistled, and the creature he'd called Ricou waddled back with curiosity toward them. Ricou stopped in front of Gabriel.

"He won't do you any harm." Cora crouched and petted the scaly monkey creature. "He's friendly."

"What is he?" Misty knelt by Cora.

"He's one of my mother's creations," Nils said. "But now I think you can just call him a pet."

"Come on," Cora said. "We'll take you back to Delia."

The creature suddenly leapt and crawled up Gabriel's arm. He perched on his shoulder, ruffling Gabriel's hair, and then down his other arm, where he latched on with spindly little green fingers to Gabriel's wristband.

"Careful," Nils intoned. "He likes new toys." Suddenly—before Gabriel could even move his other hand to try to swat him out of the way—the creature slipped the wristband off Gabriel's hand like an expert pickpocket, and dropped to the floor, moving away toward the entrance.

"Wait, I need that!" Gabriel called to the monkey creature. Peter laughed and Gabriel glared at his helmsman in exasperation.

The creature stopped and looked back, twirling the wristband on his finger.

"He was called Ricou?" Gabriel asked.

"Right," Cora said.

"Here, Ricou." Gabriel held out his hand. "I'm going to need that back." The monkey chittered with mischievous glee.

Gabriel ran after Ricou, and everyone else followed Gabriel. Ricou disappeared into a group of fruit trees.

"There!" Peter cried, pointing to the creature just long enough for Ricou to chitter at Gabriel once again.

Ricou leapt, scampering from tree to tree as they chased him.

The crew shouted up at the trees as they ran along a small sort of creek. Gabriel glancingly saw flashes of fish swimming past planters of exotic flowers and vines.

Finally they reached a little cul-de-sac. Gabriel panted, putting his hands on his knees. "You feel that?" he asked Misty. "The air is thinner." Which made sense, he thought idly. Just as at Nemolab, the air in a city beneath the sea would be kept to a minimum richness just to preserve the oxygen they produced. He'd been in California long enough that he wasn't used to it anymore.

Ricou must have pitied him, because the scaled monkey jumped and landed on Gabriel's shoulder. He touched Gabriel's hair and looked into his eyes. Ricou's eyes were as green as his skin, and full of warmth. Then he jumped up onto a wall that seemed to run the length of the park. The wall was lined with countless balconies, where Gabriel could see lights coming in behind curtains. All along the grass-and-creek level were large doors that Gabriel thought probably led up into these living areas.

They must have been close to the middle of the long park. A little way down, Gabriel saw an enormous clock tower with multiple walkways leading toward it, and then the long park went on beyond that.

Gabriel sighed. "What . . . is this?"

"This is the promenade." Nils held up his hand and pointed downward. "Ricou. Stop this. Delia will be very angry." Ricou clung to a balcony, unconvinced.

Gabriel heard rattling behind him. Peter said, "Wait." He fished something out of his pocket and held it up. He shook a little yellow bag. "Bet he's never seen this. Hey, Ricou! You want some M&M's?"

The creature stared quizzically for a moment, and then jumped, stopping not far from where Peter stood next to Misty and Gabriel. Peter crouched down and shook a couple of blue and red candies into his hand. "You want one of these?"

Ricou leaned toward Peter's hand, still holding the wristband. Gabriel wanted to lunge for it, but he thought better of it. The monkey was fast.

Ricou reached with his free hand to grab at the candies and Misty said, "Wait. We don't know if that would be safe for this creature to eat."

Nils said with a burdened sigh, "I wouldn't worry about it. He can eat pretty much anything."

"My kind of monkey," Peter said. He pushed his hand forward. Ricou took one of the candies and sniffed it, then popped it in his green scaly mouth. He smiled.

And then held out his hand for more.

"Ah." Peter closed his hand and pointed at the prize in Ricou's hand. "That. The wristband." He shook out a couple more of the candies so that there were four or five in his palm. "On the ground."

Ricou stared for a long moment. Then he dropped the wristband and snatched the candies. Gabriel picked up the wristband at once.

Just then a voice came from a balcony above. "Ricou, get up here!"

It was an older woman with her hair done up in a bun, gray ringlets at the sides of her face. While they all looked up, Ricou expertly snatched the open bag of M&M's from Peter's hand and scampered up the wall to the balcony. The woman shooed him inside past a French door and closed him in. Then she turned back to them. "Nils! Ask these folks if they want to come up."

"Nils's mother?" Misty looked at Cora.

"Delia. The greatest engineer we have ever known."

"Did she really make that creature?" Gabriel asked.

"Mm-hmm," Nils said. He seemed to soften. "Come on. She'd like to meet you."

Nils led them to a nearby door that opened as he came near. Gabriel wondered if the door got a signal in Nils's uniform or would open for anyone. They walked up three flights of the same pink coral and wood stairs, and finally reached a hallway with a door that was adorned by small planters of unrecognizable flowers.

As soon as they were there, Delia opened the door. Ricou was on her shoulder, the bag of candy in one hand as he toyed with her gray ringlets with the other. Delia embraced her son lovingly. Gabriel had known Nils now for about a quarter of an hour and already was impressed with him—duty-bound when it came to the business of the ship, kind with Cora, and now turned to mush with his mother. He seemed to be the kind of leader Gabriel would like to be.

The woman turned to Cora and the crew.

"Who in all Neptune are they?" Delia's eyes crinkled.

Cora pointed at Gabriel, jumping up and down. "He's a Nemo," she said. "A real Nemo."

"Also, we are here," Peter said with a raised hand. Delia laughed and gestured them. "Well, I've got a kettle on." They exchanged names as Delia led them to a small sitting room.

Gabriel was struck by the Victorian nature of the furniture, with a comfortable love seat and fainting couch, and wooden bric-a-brac and clocks everywhere. The adrenaline of the chase was wearing off and Gabriel finally had a chance to stop and try to bring the enormity of all that he had seen so far into his mind: He was in what seemed like a regular apartment in an underwater city that up until today he had no idea existed.

Ricou took his place on a mantel next to a black screen that had been turned off. The monkey casually lay back and stuck his hand into the packet of M&M's to pull out another candy.

"What *is* he?" Misty asked toward the kitchen Delia had disappeared into.

Delia brought back a tray of tea and cookies. They sat on the plush furniture, and Gabriel picked up one of the cookies, turning it over in his hand and sniffing it as subtly as he could.

"It's sugar," the woman said. "We grow it. What's that confection that you gave my pet, is it your own?"

"M&M's?" Peter said. "They're pretty much everywhere. They're mainly sugar, too."

"Cora called you an engineer?" Gabriel said.

The woman waggled her head. "Sure. Engineer, biologist, once I had to fix the big clock."

"Are there a lot like him?" Misty asked, nodding her head toward Ricou.

"Oh, no," Delia said. "Honestly, Ricou was kind of an accident. I try not to do too many of those."

"Accidents?" Peter asked.

"Monkeys." Delia beamed. "Nightmares if they get in the control room. Anyway, as Nils will tell you, I'm pretty much retired." She sat back, shaking her head. "So the Nemos have found us."

"Cora said something like that," Gabriel said. "I'm not...I don't quite know what it means. Did you want us to find you?"

"Who are you asking?" Delia chuckled. Then she seemed to catch herself. "I think we've always hoped that the day would come. The City of Nautilus needs its Nemos."

Gabriel looked at the French doors at the end of the room, out to the enormous promenade.

"There's so much I'd like to understand," Gabriel said. "I'm descended from the family Captain Nemo started at Lincoln Island, but all we know of what became of Nemo is that he disappeared on the last voyage of the *Nautilus* with the rest of the crew in the early 1900s. We found the *Nautilus*, which led us here. Did Captain Nemo survive to join the City?"

Delia sipped her tea. "Oh, yes. He was here in the beginning. He was the first director. Until what I think you'd call 1930."

Gabriel did some math and scoffed. "Nineteen thirty? He'd have been something like a hundred and twenty years old."

The old woman shrugged. "That was the year he left us."

Gabriel bent forward in the love seat. "Did he have more family? Children?" His mind suddenly played out the possibility that he could have living cousins in this city.

Delia looked down as if trying to remember. "None that I can think of." She reached forward, laying her hand on his. "But we are the crew of the *Nautilus*, and I promise you, we do everything to honor his memory."

Nils cleared his throat and rose, putting his hands on his mother's shoulders. "I'm afraid we don't have much time. I was going to take them to Minerva straightaway, but Ricou kind of...distracted us." He kissed her head.

Delia gave Nils a look that indicated that she was aware of how busy her son was.

Gabriel and his crew and Cora politely thanked Delia for the cookies. Peter went to the mantel and held out his fist to Ricou, who remarkably managed to pick up what Peter was laying down, and bumped back.

Nils led them to the door and looked back, waving once more at his mother.

The door whistled open and a woman was standing there in the hall. She was not as old as Delia, but she was older than Nils. She wore a leather jacket and smart cotton pants. The expression she wore was one of amusement. "Nils."

"Oh!" Nils said.

"Dr. Ramoray," the woman called. "Thank you for entertaining."

Before his mother could answer, Nils said, "Minerva, I can explain."

"Nothing to explain," she said brightly, and turned to the crew. "So you're the visitors from above."

"This is Gabriel Nemo," Cora said. "You know, the one who tamed the...Pacific."

Gabriel saw something flicker through Minerva's eyes, but she maintained her pleasant smile. She didn't seem like the commander he had been expecting. She wasn't brazen or instantly challenging like Gabriel's sister, who was always his epitome of leadership. She seemed more ... curious.

"So." Minerva looked from Gabriel to Peter and Misty. "It's you."

"IF WE'RE GOING to talk, we should do it somewhere that fits," Minerva said. Then she practically clicked her heels, indicating the stairs with her head. "Come." She led the *Kekada* crew out. Cora made as if to join them, and Minerva said with complete friendliness, "Nils, Cora, Dr. Ramoray—I'd be thrilled if you'd join us later."

So she wants to talk to us alone, Gabriel thought as Minerva led them down the stairs. That made sense, of course. They were the new ones. And yet in the past few hours since they'd picked Cora out of the ocean, he'd gotten used to having the girl with the goggles around.

Out on the promenade, Minerva walked briskly a little bit in front of them but arranged so that she could turn her head and talk.

"So you're the leader of the City?" Gabriel asked.

"I'm the director," Minerva said. "We like to think that MIM is the leader."

"*Mobilis in Mobili?*" Misty asked. "That was engraved on something we saw."

Minerva stopped as she passed a lamppost on the edge of the beige trail. It was late afternoon by Gabriel's wristband now, and the lights had shifted such that the sky was growing darker, and the lamps had come on. The post was black and swooping, curved slightly like the inside of a ship. It ran up and down with soft oval lights that looked like riveted portholes from the *Nautilus*. She lay her hand next to one of the lights, where a smaller brass oval was carved with the letters MIM.

"Yes. Change in the changes." She turned to them, clasping her hands and leaning forward. "Forward momentum. Changing the world through our thoughts and our deeds. Starting with this place. A perfect statement of our love for a world that is mostly ocean, and where people thrive when they reflect daily on its elegance and beauty." She beckoned and they began to walk. "Come."

They were headed along the tree-lined path toward the enormous clock tower. The whole tower was decorated with carved light wood. As the lighting had subtly shifted, Gabriel now saw four figureheads like those on the tower outside, lit from below in amber. The clock itself had curled, black, Victorian-style hands.

The director passed one of the round planters that lined the walkway—and froze so that the rest caught up and had to stagger to a stop. She turned, putting her hand to her chin, staring at the planter. Then she crouched as if she had never seen it before.

The planter was round, and Gabriel saw that it had a retracted hood with a hinge, he guessed so that they could close it up and move it.

"Huh," Minerva said.

"Ma'am?" Gabriel asked.

Minerva frowned slightly and stayed crouched, waving her arms to someone Gabriel hadn't noticed, a man in a leather jacket and a dark gray painter's cap who was working at a panel against the wall about fifty feet away. "MIMgineer!"

Peter muttered, "MIMgineer?"

The guy hustled over. "Director."

Minerva gestured downward. "I just had a ... here, come down, I just had a thought. What do you see when you look at this?" She now held her long fingers under a large, shiny rivet that made the joint where the hood of the planter would come up to close it.

The guy took off the cap as he crouched. "Ah well, that's a standard medium planter hinge, I think it's item SMP-2-L, left because that's the left one from the orientation of the plan..."

She waved that away. "But what do you *see*?"

"A . . . hinge?"

"I understand," Minerva said solemnly, even a little sadly. She gestured to the others to come down to her level. Now there were five people crouched and staring at the planter. "I do. I've looked at this planter or hundreds like it along the promenade every day and I didn't realize until now how much it was sapping our energy to have it be this way."

"Sapping your energy?" Gabriel asked.

"The hinge has this bright, ugly bolt that says, I'm here to make the hinge work, but I don't care, really. But MIM is in changing these things. Finding new ways to care, every day." She gestured with both her hands, scooping out from her chest as if handing over her own heart. "If we were to reengineer this so that the rivet were somehow inside, so that the whole planter would just appear to close as if it were a peapod closing back up, can you see how that would be more MIM?" She looked back at Gabriel with a wink. "More Nemo?"

The man's face reflected something like euphoria. "Absolutely. Yes. Absolutely, we can do that."

"That would be excellent." Minerva put her hand on the man's shoulder. "Let's get them on the promenade in two weeks."

Minerva sprang up and gestured again, and they began to walk.

"That was amazing," Gabriel said quietly to Misty and Peter. "Did you see how expertly she did that? She just came up with an idea and it's going to happen."

"Not a bad idea," Peter said. "I think I know how they can make that hinge."

"The point isn't that we know how to make the hinge," Minerva said brightly. "The point is we never noticed we *could*."

The crewmembers followed her to the clock tower and Minerva stopped before a great door. It swept open, and they entered a wide room that reminded Gabriel of the bridge of a ship. There were multiple stations and sonar screens, and cotton-dressed, leather-jacketed officers in goggles at work. It was softly lit, just well enough to see everything clearly, but not harsh. Gabriel saw many of the officers swiping in the air. "I think they're using holographic menus," he said.

"Cool," Peter said.

"This is the command center," Minerva said, but she was leading them on. "But that's not what I want to show you."

"We'd love to see it," Misty said as they went through a door. "Which one of those sections is ops? How many different systems are you running?"

"Time for all that later," Minerva said as they began to climb the stairs. "Come."

They reached a landing with a door that said DIRECTOR—MIM, which Gabriel took to be Minerva's own area, like his own library when they'd had the *Obscure*.

"We could keep climbing," Minerva said wryly, "but rank has its privileges." She opened the door and they all shuffled through.

And found themselves in the inner sanctum of the *Nautilus*.

Or something very like it, but larger and newer and sculpted to fit its owner. There was a pipe organ behind an enormous desk, and great screens on curved walls, each displaying the world outside the City—whales and fish and turtles. Old naval paintings hung at a slight distance from the walls. An enormous conference table appeared to float in the air, though at a second glance with a little crouch, Gabriel could see supports toward the center.

Gabriel spun around and laughed. She was living on the *Nautilus*. "This is . . . *amazing*."

Peter cleared his throat. "You'll have to excuse the captain. He is very excitable, which is absolutely something I say all the time."

Misty snorted, then got serious. "Director, this really is very impressive."

"Oh, this isn't where we're going," Minerva said. "Come, come." And they walked to the end of the room. On the wall at the corner was a painting of a ship, and above it an oval brass plaque that said LIFT. Another one to their right, Gabriel noticed, said DESTINY.

Minerva pressed LIFT, a door in the wall swooped back, and they entered the lift, which glowed with amber. The outer wall of the lift looked right out on the promenade, and they began to rise.

Gabriel looked out to see the path leading to the tower as it wound through the promenade and the high cliffs of balcony after balcony. "This lift is opaque on the outside to look like the wood of the tower."

"Yes," Minerva said, her eyes full of mirth.

When the lift stopped, they were at the top of the City. They stepped back out into a great room with clear walls all around, so that in each direction they looked out through the hands of a face of the clock. The room itself was empty, with bare cherry-colored wood floors.

"Where are the gears?" Peter asked.

"This clock has been a digital display since I was a teen," Minerva said. "Your friend Delia programmed it. Now this is just an observation deck."

Minerva walked toward the face of the clock. The second hand swept slowly around, as thick as Gabriel's body. He could see the promenade disappearing.

"How big is this promenade?" He turned around and looked back in the other direction.

"The size of the City," Minerva said. "But let me show you something."

She pulled a white controller from her pocket and held it before her, and Gabriel heard a faint click.

One of the walls went opaque, filled with an image of the long black *Nautilus*. "This is where we *came* from."

"Oh, look, a slideshow," Peter muttered. "It's like a Nemo fever."

"Yes!" Misty stepped toward the wall. "We found the *Nautilus*. And we found clues on it that led us to . . . this part of the world, anyway."

"I have to compliment you on your tenacity," Minerva said. "But yes. We had to leave—I mean, the original crew did. This would have been my great-grandfather and the rest." Minerva shrugged. "We had to abandon the ship. There was poison in the air. Captain Nemo had prepared an evacuation ship, and in that we made our escape." *We*, Gabriel noticed. Not *they*. Minerva talked about the original crew as though they were still alive.

"This is it." She indicated the screen, which now showed a long ship aside the *Nautilus* made up of what looked like rubber, or maybe . . .

"Is that ship made of whale skin?" Gabriel guessed.

"Well, it was made from a cloth devised from the genetic code of whales," Minerva said. "It was called *Exnautilus*. It was large enough for the crew and the needed rations. An electrical current unfolded and solidified the ship, and it served us well."

"But you were on the other side of the world," Misty said. "Why would you come all the way to Tiger Bay?"

"There's a lot to that," Minerva said, "but Captain Nemo had allies and we were to rendezvous with them. Which we did. And thus we had people enough for our new world away from the world."

They spun around as another wall lit up to show an enormous shipyard. "We worked in secret on an island off the coast of Wales. This took several years. Building."

Gabriel grimaced. "To do what? This is an underwater *city*. How did you build an underwater city in 1911? Did you build it and then sink it?"

"*Sink* it?" Minerva laughed. "No. My goodness. Heavens, no."

Now Minerva clicked again, and another wall showed a map of the oceans. The map showed a pink line that stretched, crawling about the ocean, from South America to North America, around the Arctic, to Bristol Channel. "This is our activity of the past two years."

"So, you haven't stayed here," Gabriel said. "Where do you go when you leave the City? Do you have a ship?"

"Gabriel! Captain Nemo, I should say. It's so amazing to hear that name. There is no need to *leave Dinas Nautilus*." Minerva smiled. "*Dinas Nautilus is* a ship."

"*What?*" Misty whispered before Gabriel could get the word out. It was impossible. A ship this large, on the bottom of the ocean, moving? With the citizens picking grapes, watering plants on their balconies, walking up and down a lamplit promenade in their strange, leather-and-frills clothing. It had to be...

Gabriel shivered and laughed. Everything about it was... Yes, this was what happened when *Mobilis in Mobili* just kept on *Mobil-ing*. You didn't hide in a lab. You built another *Nautilus* and you went forward. But the size of it!

"If what you say is true," he said, "the *Dinas Nautilus* would have to be the largest submarine the world has ever known."

Minerva opened her arms and turned to look through the clock. "By far."

"I'm trying to imagine the engines it takes to lift this city—this ship," Peter said. "Can we see the engine rooms?"

"You can see anything," Minerva said. "Nils was right that I'd like to show you what we've done to honor the Nemo legacy. Your timing is actually really excellent. We're preparing for Destiny Day, and you'll definitely want to be part of that."

"Destiny Day?" Gabriel asked. "What's that?"

"It sounds really MIM, whatever it is," Peter said.

Minerva clapped her hands and hunched forward again, a thing that he had come to expect from her when she was inviting people into her thoughts. It was stunning how well she brought you in. "Destiny Day is actually something we wanted to talk to you about. I mean, you're honored guests. I can only—"

An alarm blared, echoing around the room. Through the glass of the clock, the light changed all down the promenade, filtering red as bells rang loudly. They were not the klaxons that Gabriel heard on a Nemoship, but old-fashioned metal alarm bells. The crew looked at one another, suddenly tense. They were used to springing into action. Gabriel wished they were aboard the *Kekada*—he didn't like hearing an alarm and having no idea what to look at or respond to.

"Director?" a voice came from somewhere in the ceiling.

Minerva responded, walking to the wall to look out. "Yes."

"We're in danger of being discovered."

10

THEY HURRIED TO the command center, which Gabriel realized really *was* the bridge of an enormous ship. The chatter of many voices came to his ears. A sonar circle took up a huge viewscreen, the bright hand circling around and lighting up a large image near the ship. The shape of the *Dinas Nautilus* took up nearly a quarter of the screen from the center.

"What is it?" Minerva asked. All business now, like a different person.

An officer looked over at her and nodded at the *Kekada* crew. "It's a submarine."

"How big?"

"About three hundred and fifty feet," a man in gold epaulettes said.

"It's not the *Nebula*," Misty murmured to Gabriel, and he nodded. His sister Nerissa's ship was five hundred feet long. And as much as he wanted to see her, he was glad this strange arriving sub wasn't her—if she showed up before he let the *Dinas Nautilus* know he had shared their coordinates, there might be some explaining to do. But this outside was someone else.

"Three-fifty feet?" Peter repeated. "It could be British. The Astute class ships are that length, a little less, I think."

"What are they doing?" Minerva asked.

The officer who'd spoken before, a broad-shouldered man with a beard, said, "They came in from the south. We thought they were just passing through on maneuvers. But then they turned. Now they're just hanging there. Using active sonar." Active sonar was the process by which submarines created a map of the sea around them, sending out a ping of sound and catching it as it bounced back. It was audible to other ships, so it also meant that so far, the submarine did not behave as though it was in danger. If it were worried, it would probably kill its own sonar and go silent.

"Have they seen us?"

"Probably not," the officer said. "They're still far enough away, and we're sitting on the bottom. We probably look like nothing at all on sonar. But if they get closer, they'll be able to tell we're a construction."

"Let's see them," Minerva said.

The sonar screen moved to the bottom right corner,

and the rest of the screen switched to a powerful camera view.

A great ship, flat along its body and tapered at the nose, moved very slowly a few hundred feet off the ocean floor. It was a mile away, creeping toward the aft section of the *Dinas Nautilus*. But more than this, a high beam from its nose swept slowly back and forth before it. It had lit up the landing squares that the *Kekada* had come down on just earlier.

"What are you?" Minerva asked the screen.

"It's not British," Peter said, and the officers turned toward him. "It has some of the features of an Astute class, but *look* at it." He stepped forward and drew his fingers across the air toward the viewscreen. The sail, the tall head of a submarine, had a sort of wavelike design that flowed backward. "The curved sail is odd, and it's ringed with windows—those have to be incredibly strong to withstand the pressure down here. Naval ships don't use them. And there are three stabilizer fins on each side. That's different from any navy."

"I don't see any markings," the helmsman—for so Gabriel had come to think of the bearded man—said.

"We can't see the top of the nose," Gabriel said. But already the skin was tingling on the back of his neck. "Do you have a higher camera?"

"Yes," Minerva said. "Show me the tower camera."

The image switched, and now they were looking down

at a greater distance, nearly a thousand feet from the ship as it crawled through the water toward them. Gabriel saw the mark on the top of the nose instantly. A circle around a great *M*.

Gabriel exchanged glances with Misty and Peter, and they all said, "Maelstrom."

Minerva clapped her hand down on the ledge below the viewscreen. "We don't have time for this."

"What do you know about the Maelstrom?" Gabriel asked.

Nils came in just then, answering as he entered. "They're pirates. They steal technology. I don't think they know about *Dinas Nautilus*, but we've lost equipment, small craft to them."

"That explains why so much of their tech is kind of like ours," Misty said. Maelstrom had long been pledged to make war on the Nemos, and they exhibited amazing technology that the Nemos had always thought might be based on Nemotech. But now Gabriel realized that much of it could be based on the technology of *Dinas Nautilus* as well.

"Is it strange for them to get this close?"

Minerva turned to Gabriel, running a hand through her curly hair. "They never have before."

Gabriel winced. Maelstrom had strange ways of spying on the Nemos. He wondered if they had been tracking the *Kekada*.

"Do we engage?" the helmsman asked.

Gabriel knew what his sister would have said: *Blow these guys out of the water.* He was close to feeling that way himself. Maelstrom had kidnapped his mom, and he couldn't forgive that. But, in the end, the sailors of Maelstrom were people. Sure, they were serving a master who terrorized the seas, but he wouldn't suggest simply murdering them. Couldn't. It wasn't in his nature. Still the voice of his sister in his head was hard to keep silent.

"Don't engage," Nils said. "We need to move."

"*Move?*" Minerva snarled. "We've only *been* here five months. If we move it throws off the entire migration plan. Are we supposed to stay in the next spot twice as long? We have these plans for a reason."

"Of course," Nils said. He held up both hands, patting the air as if to placate Minerva. "But if we engage them, if we hit them with something, especially if we blow them up," Nils said calmly, "their comrades will know. And they'll trace us. They may be communicating already. Look at them right now—they're just searching. They're curious. But they haven't seen *us* yet. Ma'am, we need to move. And we need to do it now."

"If they see us moving, they'll follow," Minerva said. "We need to hit them."

"Just think of the risk," Nils said. "How long would you need to get aloft and away?"

Gabriel turned to Misty and Peter, keeping his voice low. "What do *you* think?"

"I think they're gonna fight one way or the other, and they'll need help," Misty whispered back.

Minerva looked up at the sonar screen, which showed a map of the many twists and turns. She shook her head. Like she was running down all the possibilities to conclude that Nils was right. "They're moving slowly because they're *searching*, but they'll be here soon enough." She looked at Nils. "We'll need ten minutes. To lift off and get far enough into these canyons that the Maelstrom can't know where we went—if they even know we were here at all."

"Ten minutes? The pilots of the Watch can do it," Nils said. "We need to get out in small craft. So that we can swarm—and distract them from the City while you make your escape."

Peter was listening and whispered back to Gabriel and Misty, "Come on, we don't really know these guys."

Gabriel understood where Peter was coming from. They *didn't* know the *Dinas Nautilus* very well. But he knew who the bad guys were. "We know the Maelstrom—a lot better than they do. Isn't that enough? I feel pretty okay about ruining their day."

Minerva put her hand on Nils's shoulder. "Then it's settled. Ten minutes." She turned and spoke to the tactical officer. "Smoke screen. Then prepare the City for voyage."

Misty asked Nils, "What does *smoke screen* mean?"

"Smoke screen, aye," another officer called, hitting a series of buttons.

"We're going to surround the City with a thick cloud of silt," Nils said.

Minerva nodded. Then she turned to the *Kekada* crew, adopting again some of the bright tone that she'd been using before. "You three? You'll need to find someplace safe. There are four gazebos in the promenade, each with safety seats. I recommend you go there."

"They could go back to my mother's," Nils said. "She has emergency seating next to her lab."

Gabriel held up a hand. "Ma'am? The *Kekada* can fall in with the Watch."

Minerva gave it a moment's thought and then nodded. "Very well."

"Excellent," Nils said, clapping his hand on Gabriel's shoulder. "Then it's time to get to the hangar."

"Smoke screen active," someone called.

Suddenly on the viewscreen, hundreds of plumes of silt burst from the ocean floor around the edges of the *Dinas Nautilus*. The plumes swirled into the water, blanketing the floor and flowing all around the Maelstrom ship. From the eye of the tower, a whole undulating layer of silt—liquid dust, basically—covered everything for a quarter mile.

"Heavy sonar," Minerva called. "We have to see through all this. Retract tower and prepare the City."

Gabriel heard clanging bells warbling in the distance. Onscreen, the camera at the top of the tower was lowering smoothly, as the whole tower dropped in on itself.

An officer went to a panel on the wall where a cream-colored glass cone jutted out at the end of a ribbed metal arm. He grabbed the cone and twisted it down to his mouth.

"Citizens," he said, "prepare for voyage. Batten down all personal effects. Secure pets and cover all liquids. Retire to safety and mind all children. Time to liftoff... three hundred seconds."

Nils started leading them out the door and into the promenade. He tapped his belt. "Cora, this is Nils."

Cora's voice came on, tinny and distant. "Yes?"

"We're headed for the hangar. We'll need you to crew your parents' old ship. Head for the *Valencia*."

11

AS THEY RAN, Gabriel saw citizens running for the doorways. The black planters lining the walkways that Minerva had asked one of the MIMgineers to redesign closed themselves: the plants retracted with their soil a few inches, then the lids of the planters swept up over the plants, and then the entire planter lowered straight down and out of sight, leaving only a slight dome that in turn glowed to provide emergency path indicators. Above Gabriel's head, the balconies closed up as shields lowered over each one. Each shield that dropped over the balconies clanged loudly, so that as they ran toward the hangar with hundreds of balconies clapping shut, the metal sound filled the whole atrium. Next to the walkways, metal covers slid over the streams, fish disappearing from view.

Not far above him, Gabriel saw a dog stick its head out and bark several times as the shield came down. A pair of small hands grabbed it and pulled it in, and the metal slammed shut.

Cora caught up with them out of nowhere. "Delia is strapped in," she said to Nils.

Nils pursed his lips thankfully. They reached the hangar doors and stopped. The double doors opened. "*Dinas Nautilus* will be lifting off as soon as all their engines are online."

"What's the plan?" Misty asked.

"We're going to distract the Maelstrom," Nils said. "Keep them occupied while the City slips away. It's the best we can do."

"Just distract?" Peter smirked. "You don't mean fight?"

"Distract," Nils said as they ran into the hangar. "The City will have its smoke screen and its counter-sonar activated, but we need to keep the Maelstrom occupied. *Dinas Nautilus* has to disappear like a ghost in the night."

Four more pilots in jackets and epaulettes fell in with them and started heading for the various craft that were arranged around the wide, dark room. "But we'll see what happens. We stay with the Maelstrom until the City is far enough away that we can break off and follow safely."

Inside, the floor was still slick from where it had been flooded when they came in. Gabriel slipped once as they ran toward their ships, but not Cora, whose heavy and rubberized boot soles were built for slick tile.

Cora headed for a two-person ship that flickered with greenish scales similar to the ones on the *Bluefin*. She turned back. "Does one of you want to join me on the *Valencia*?"

They were headed toward the *Kekada* and Misty held up a hand. "I'll go. Gabriel, can you ..."

"Handle weapons?" Gabriel finished her thought. "Yes."

As Cora and Misty neared it, the canopy of the *Valencia* popped open. Gabriel watched the pair climb aboard as Peter lowered the *Kekada* a couple of inches until he could trigger the iris underneath. Then they crawled up one at a time.

In the bridge, Peter jumped to his station, putting on his headphones with one hand while he powered up the engines with the other. "Main power," he said as the *Kekada* started to hum. Gabriel took Misty's chair.

On the screen the camera showed the doors of the hangar closing as the canopy came down over the two-person *Valencia*. "We're ready," Gabriel said. His body hummed with anticipation.

"Maelstrom, man," Peter said. "I kind of got used to not having them around."

"Me, too." The last time they had seen a Maelstrom ship, it had been pursuing the wounded *Obscure* to the bottom of the ocean. Gabriel was still angry that they had put his family in danger and destroyed his ship. He wanted to meet them in the water.

"Flood the hangar," Nils called. Outside, he could see Nils in a two-man ship not far from Cora and Misty's *Valencia*. "Watch, stand by."

Water began to flood into the hangar from the slats along the walls. Gabriel watched the water rise over the *Valencia* and the other ships, and soon it was passing their own camera. They were underwater now, the *Valencia* waiting just ahead of them. The hollow sound of machinery rose around them, and the floor under them was lifting off, raising them through the hangar. The *Valencia* on its own elevator looked like the head of a drowned trophy as it moved up toward a slot in the top of the hangar.

Shortly the shell of the hangar passed them, and they were up on the roof, the elevator clacking into place as they stopped atop the hull of the *Dinas Nautilus*.

The water swirled with silt and he could see the *Valencia* no more. "Peter, sonar."

The sonar screen snapped into view, but it was blanketed with meaningless snow. "I can't see anything."

"Adjusting," Peter said.

"All this silt." Gabriel shook his head. "Can our engines handle this?"

"The filters should handle it," Peter said. They had made modifications to all the Nemoships' engine filters since they'd started spending so much time in the Great Pacific Garbage Patch. This was a field thousands of miles wide in the north and middle of the Pacific Ocean. It was the result of decades of trash finding its way through natural ocean currents to one swirling area, where the plastic ground down to tiny pellets that choked animals and fouled even the advanced engines of the Nemos. "I *hope*, anyway."

The sonar screen crackled with static and then popped into a grainy, poor resolution. He could see the shape of the tower, which was now just a knob atop the body of the *Dinas Nautilus*. He saw the shape that represented the *Valencia* moving swiftly to the side, away from the main body. Directly south, at the bottom of the screen, the Maelstrom ship lit up yellow. But there was noise everywhere.

"Make our elevation fifty feet off the floor," Gabriel said. "Move us starboard, get us out toward the side of the canyon. I don't want to be over the City when it starts to rise."

"Aye," Peter said. Jets in the walls chugged, emptying out liquid as outer jets pushed downward, lifting them off the floor. "Retracting legs." The legs clacked into place below them as Peter swung the *Kekada* around toward the edge.

Gabriel saw five other ships besides *Kekada* and *Valencia* zip out, forming up briefly in a line. Two of them swooped up and fell back near the City while the rest went forward.

"Pilots of the Watch," came Nils's voice over the intercom. "Let's get the Maelstrom's attention and stay out of one another's way. We're going to swarm, but we're going to go in order. Keep a constant distance of at least thirty yards from one another. First order is to move straight over their nose, then to port, then cross them again to starboard. If the ship ahead of you went over, you go under, and vice versa. Cross, and cross, and cross, until you reach the end, then begin again. My ship will begin the run, watch your sonar for your turn if you don't have a visual. Do not fire unless fired upon. Energy weapons only."

Energy weapons. So like the *Kekada*, the other ships would be using torpedoes programmed to knock the Maelstrom ship out. Assuming all the usual risks.

One by one, each of the *Dinas* ships sounded off their understanding, including Cora, who spoke for the craft holding her and Misty.

"Copy," Gabriel spoke into the intercom. He kept the channel open.

On the sonar screen, through all the noise he could see the shape of the City was shifting. It grew larger as the silt covering much of the hull flowed away. It was lifting off. Peter yanked the stick and moved them farther away.

"*Dinas Nautilus* is lifting off," Peter said. "Time to give 'em room."

"Sonar's a mess—split screen, show me the silt," Gabriel said. He wanted a visual, any visual. The sonar screen took the left half while the cameras took up the right, plumes of silt whipping around them as they flew through the water.

Gabriel looked at the sonar and felt a moment of disorientation and even fear. Including the Maelstrom's giant sub, there were seven ships in the water, and the lumps on the sonar screen were fuzzy and almost useless. "Oh boy."

"What?" Peter looked over at him.

"This is gonna be a little new, this many ships around at once. I'd feel a lot more comfortable in the *Obscure*."

"You and me both, buddy," Peter said. "But Nils's plan makes sense. We'll seem to be all over the incoming ship but if each of us is doing all this in order, we should avoid being in the same place at once. Emphasis on *should*."

And then Nils began his first run, his little ship spinning straight toward the Maelstrom ship, missing at the last minute to swoop to the starboard. The next ship lined up as Nils's ship zoomed under the Maelstrom ship and flew toward the other side.

All this driving of submarines around other submarines was dangerous. Every single ship was airtight, and it had two enemies: the other ships, and the water. The whole point of a submarine battle was to keep water out of your own vessel, and every nearby obstacle, whether a torpedo or another ship, was deadly. And Nils's plan demanded the constant threat of collision, even if they did try to overcome it by sticking to Nils's choreography.

The fifth DN ship to fly toward the Maelstrom intruders was the *Valencia* with Cora and Misty. Gabriel couldn't see them through the silt at all. They were a blob on the sonar screen, moving fast. Gabriel wished he had his whole crew with him, because just then he was thinking how surely, surely this was not the kind of vacation Misty's parents had in mind for her. And then the *Valencia* was swooping over the nose of the Maelstrom ship.

It was their turn. "All right," Gabriel said into the intercom. "*Kekada* making its approach." He clicked it off and called for an intercept course.

"Aye, intercept course," Peter said. The great thing about a ship like the *Kekada* was they could turn on a dime. They were twice as wide as the *Valencia*, but they were still barely as wide as the Maelstrom ship. It was like zipping toward a paper towel roll on a quarter.

Proximity alarms rang out and Peter clapped them down with a touch.

"Two hundred feet off the deck," Peter reported.

"Full speed," Gabriel said.

They flew onward, the engines chugging. Shortly they could see a shape—a great shadow in the brown silt. It was the Maelstrom ship. Its high beam was a broken ribbon of light in the silt.

"Down," Gabriel said.

Peter shoved the stick forward and they dropped, fast, slipping through the silt and flying along underneath the body of the Maelstrom ship. They were close enough that even in the silt they could see the panels of metal and the rivets glistening along the ship's seams.

On the sonar screen, six ships were swarming, following a nearly identical course. The people inside the large submarine must be going insane with alarm klaxons and worry that they were about to be torpedoed.

"We're halfway down along their body," Gabriel said. "Break to port, out, around, back to starboard, then when you reach the end of the long sub, head straight back."

"Aye." Peter sent them spinning away and they sped through the water, leaving the curtains of silt behind for green open ocean. He sped up the *Kekada* and they punched through the curtain of silt, suddenly awash in brown columns again. Peter brought them sailing back over the top, so close that if he'd let the *Kekada*'s robot legs hang down, they would have scraped the Maelstrom's hull.

"Look out!" called a voice on the intercom.

Someone had gotten confused. Another *Dinas* ship burst through the silt and banked suddenly to avoid hitting the *Kekada*. Gabriel's hair fell straight back as Peter yanked the stick and the *Kekada* zipped up at ninety degrees.

"Hang on," Peter said, and they curled back, upside down for a moment, and then spun again, swooping back down to hurtle toward the Maelstrom.

"Well *that* was cool," Misty called. For a moment the *Valencia* came into view, crossing the ship, and the *Kekada* fell in behind them.

"Nothin' to it," Peter said, but he was smiling. The smile dropped as an alarm rang out. "Torpedo in the water!"

From the nose of the Maelstrom ship, a missile shot out, showing on the sonar screen as a bright light that flew out and was making its way back toward the *Kekada*.

"Evasive," Gabriel said. Peter sped up the *Kekada* and then jerked up at an angle, moving back toward the Maelstrom ships. The torpedo whistled past them, and Gabriel watched it fly right over the viewscreen, losing itself in the silt.

Peter pointed at the sonar. "Look. The City is moving."

On the screen, the vast *Dinas Nautilus* was up and slowly beginning to drag itself forward in the ocean. It was moving so slowly it was almost impossible to tell it was moving at all.

"Was that a torpedo?" Misty called.

"Yes," Gabriel said.

"Nils, free to engage?" Cora called.

"Affirmative," Nils's voice came back. "Engage at will." He was true to his order. Nils was in the middle of a run toward the Maelstrom's nose and unleashed a pincer torpedo that shot through the water over the body of the long ship.

"What power setting are we using?" Misty called.

Cora shot back, "Set power, fifty percent."

Gabriel knew what Misty was thinking. Of course the weapons on the *Kekada* were pincer energy, usually intended to wound a ship. They had no idea how powerful the energy weapons on the DN ships really were. But he was a little thrilled to see his own crewmate so perfectly slot into someone else's ship. It made him feel like they'd all been making progress.

"Torpedo away," Misty said. On the sonar screen, through the snow, the *Valencia* shot from below to move along the body of the Maelstrom ship.

"Torpedo in the water, *Valencia*'s," Peter cried. A missile dropped from the *Valencia* and shot toward the prow of the Maelstrom ship. The *Valencia* hauled up, moving straight upward away from it.

Sparkles lit up on the sonar screen as the Maelstrom ship shot out some kind of countermeasures, which flew around the nose. The torpedoes Misty and Nils had shot exploded over the enemy ship as they hit the countermeasures, and the silt lit up with crackles of energy.

"It's amazing how close that is to pincer energy," Gabriel said.

"It makes sense," Peter said as he piloted. "All of us—this crew, the *Dinas Nautilus*, and the Maelstrom have been adapting from Nemo for years. We're more alike than different."

The Maelstrom ship shuddered, rising in the water and moving to its port. "Maelstrom torpedo," Peter shouted.

The missile was headed for the *Valencia* this time, and Cora twisted the *Valencia*'s path, corkscrewing upward to evade the torpedo. It kept coming.

"Countermeasures, let's help her out," Gabriel cried.

"You're the one with the button," Peter called.

"Yep," Gabriel said, firing countermeasures toward the *Valencia*. The little canisters broke off from one another and whipped through the water like bees, creating a cloud on the sonar screen. As the *Valencia* pulled away, the torpedo caught in the *Kekada*'s countermeasures and exploded.

The impact sent a shock wave through the water that shook the *Kekada*.

"Move us up and come around again, prepare to fire," Gabriel said as the *Kekada* pushed up, the bridge tilting back.

"*Dinas Nautilus* is picking up speed," Nils said.

Peter was watching the sonar and said to Gabriel, "It's still barely to the end of this canyon." The image of *Dinas Nautilus* moving was so faint it could have been a ghost in the image. But they were taking too much time for the enormous ship to pick up speed.

The *Kekada* came around again, moving through the silt. Gabriel asked Peter, "You want to try to drag them away?"

"You bet."

"Nils," Gabriel called, "I'd like to drive the Maelstrom toward the surface just to buy a little more time and distance. Can you cover the City's retreat?"

Nils came back, "Absolutely."

"Peter, when we fire, raise elevation five hundred feet."

"Five hundred, aye."

"Cora? You hear that, we're luring them up."

"Copy," she said.

Through the silt the Maelstrom ship showed itself again and Gabriel didn't hesitate to slap the console. "Torpedo away."

The missile shot out from below the viewscreen and headed for the hull of the Maelstrom ship, and then it wasn't visible anymore because Peter was taking them steeply toward the surface. Gabriel felt himself shoved hard against his seat as they pushed upward, the engines churning.

The missile exploded somewhere below them. "It was a miss," Gabriel said. "The Maelstrom ship is elevating—they're coming after us. How's *Dinas* doing?"

"Gone," Peter said. "It'll look like the Maelstrom came across some deep-water base or something and got chased by some ships."

"Good," Gabriel said. "Now the Maelstrom is our problem."

"Torpedo in the water!" Peter cried. "You have a weird idea of good."

"Evasive," Gabriel said. "Depth?"

"Seventy-five feet," Peter said.

Peter whipped them to the side. The torpedo screamed past them, proximity alarms ringing out. Peter whipped the ship around and for a moment they went inverted again, the torpedo disappearing as it flew underneath the roof of the *Kekada* and away.

"*Valencia?*" Gabriel called as they leveled out again. "I want to get us out of here."

Onscreen, the Maelstrom ship was away and curving around to come after the *Valencia*, which was between the Maelstrom ship and the *Kekada*.

"I'm out of torpedoes," Cora called. The Maelstrom ship was bearing down on her and Misty. That wasn't good. All the *Valencia* could do now was avoid getting hit.

"Peter, pursue the Maelstrom ship. *Valencia*, head toward the surface and then get behind us. Peter, I'm hitting Maelstrom, full power." A fully charged pincer torpedo might well short out the entire Maelstrom ship.

But before he could, Peter cried out "Torpedo!" again. It whistled under the *Valencia*, which spun out of the way—but just barely. The torpedo blew up in the water.

Gabriel's mouth hung open in horror as the starboard wing of the *Valencia* cracked, sending the little ship tumbling.

"We're out of control," Cora said.

"Can you make the surface?" Gabriel asked.

"We're trying," Misty said, her voice jittering as the *Valencia* shook in the water.

"Your depth is twenty feet," Gabriel called. "Eject!" At twenty feet, they could swim for it. No depth sickness at twenty feet. At twenty feet you could survive.

"Ejecting!" Cora shouted. On the viewscreen the spinning *Valencia* split open, the canopy tumbling away as Cora's and Misty's chairs whooshed up on rockets into the water. Gabriel watched the chairs break apart into small floating bits that ballooned up, and Cora and Misty were yanked by the shoulders up toward the surface.

"Pick them up," Gabriel ordered.

"Captain, the Maelstrom ship is bearing down on us."

"Onscreen," Gabriel said. The rear cameras showed the flat point of the Maelstrom's nose coming up fast. He fired. "Torpedo away." The Maelstrom ship was half a mile away and the missile twisted toward it.

"They're firing countermeasures," Peter said. In the distance they saw the torpedo explode. The Maelstrom ship kept coming.

"Cora, Misty, status?" Gabriel called.

"We're on the surface," Misty said, coughing.

"Gabe," Peter said. "Maelstrom's gonna ram us." He turned to look at Gabriel. "They're one quarter mile away and closing."

"Cora and Misty are on the surface, Nils," Gabriel said. "Help them."

"They can float, I think you need it first," Nils said. "Watch, engage."

The sonar screen lit up with torpedoes from each of the small ships. They crackled against the nose of the Maelstrom ship, and on the cameras, Gabriel could see the arcs of energy dance along the Maelstrom's hull.

The Maelstrom ship stopped accelerating, and it was now drifting toward them in the water.

"Let's go get Misty and Cora," Gabriel said.

Peter pushed for the surface. The Maelstrom ship was turning slowly, using whatever auxiliary power it had left, as the fighter ships zipped across it.

"That's right," Nils said. "Time to run away. Gabriel? We're going to pursue the City. We'll see you when you get there."

Peter flipped on an image from the top cameras. It showed Misty and Cora swimming above them, two silhouettes barely visible. It was night. He came up right next to them and within minutes, Gabriel was up on the roof. Misty and Cora climbed out of the water, dropping the straps of their flotation devices and trudging across the top of the *Kekada*. Gabriel waited for them to drop through the iris and then dropped down after them.

Peter whooped and rose up, and they each gave Misty a hug, and Cora one for good measure, as the girls dripped all over the bridge.

"How do you like those fighters?" Peter asked. The *Kekada* swayed as it floated on the surface. "Maybe we could get one, Gabe."

Misty went straight to the cooler and fished out a bottle of water, opening one for Cora as well. "It needs a cooler."

The intercom crackled. "*Nebula* to *Kekada*." It was Gabriel's sister.

"Nerissa!" Gabriel was surprised to hear from her but thrilled just the same. He grabbed a bottle of water and opened it. "Boy, you will not *believe*—"

"I'm thirty miles from your position," she said, all business. "Gabe, some damaged Maelstrom jokers just ran into a cruise ship."

Gabriel was taking a sip and jerked the bottle away. "What?"

Misty ran to her station, putting on her headset. "Uh, yes, there's an SOS. Collision. There's a cruise ship sinking. Fifteen miles west of here."

"Nerissa, we just saw that Maelstrom," Gabriel said. They must have managed to pick up speed and then, without their usual equipment, or maybe in sheer disregard, slammed into another ship as they fled. "We damaged them."

"All right," Nerissa said. No admonishment. Just the situation. "We're on opposite sides of the sinking vessel. I'll meet you there."

Gabriel looked at the others. "Are you sure? You're supposed to stay hidden." Nerissa wasn't as secretive as *Dinas Nautilus*, but she was close.

"Are you kidding?" Nerissa answered. "Your ship is so small it can barely hold your crew. We'll see you."

Nerissa signed off and Peter set the course.

Gabriel said, "Fifteen miles. How fast if we go at our lowest SC speed?"

"Six minutes," Peter said. "But we could overshoot the passenger ship, or worse, if we're off a tick we could wind up miles away—or worse we could shoot *through* them."

Cora winced. "Really?"

"Well, it's something to think about." Peter frowned.

"The *Nebula* doesn't have SC drive," Misty said. "We'd get there before them."

"If it can help with the rescue, do it," Gabriel said. "Cora, you can take the science station." He indicated the other chair to the left of the front viewscreen and Cora took the seat.

Peter nodded. He looked at Cora. "That's why he's the captain. He gets to make the crazy calls. SC drive, two hundred knots." Gabriel felt the *Kekada*'s legs locking further in place as his safety belts clapped around him and he was pressed back against the seat back.

"I'm glad we're doing this on your ship," Cora said.

"Oh?" Gabriel looked over at her.

"We're not supposed to rescue," she said.

"But," Misty said, "don't you do it all the time?"

"Just like you," she said.

"Yeah, you are," Peter said with a smile. The water on the outside turned into a blur as they shot through the ocean.

12

WHALES APPEARED ALONGSIDE them and then disappeared in a blue blur as they whisked through the water. "Oil platform," Peter said, and suddenly they bent sideways, the *Kekada* going lateral as it slid around a large concrete platform. When he straightened out again, he called, "There she is."

"Disengage," Gabriel called and the *Kekada* came out of SC drive, zooming at a regular fifty knots toward the surface. The front camera showed the dark skies through the waves before they punched through, landing on the surface.

"*Nebula*, this is *Kekada*, how far away are you?"

"Fifteen minutes," Nerissa said.

"Ugh, it's raining," Gabriel said. On the screen, the

view of the night was murky as sheets of gray rain fell, droplets flowing down the camera of the drone as it hung in the air. Through the water they could see a ship of about three stories listing to the starboard, smoke belching from somewhere just above the waterline. It was about two hundred yards away. The view zoomed in and Misty read aloud the markings.

"It looks like a medium-sized cruise ship," Peter said.

"*Bruno III.*" Misty tapped a few keys and then said, "It's a Dutch cruise ship that crosses half the Atlantic, does some river cruises. Seven hundred passengers."

"Figure three crew for every ten passengers," Gabriel said.

"So that's thirty percent." Misty bit her lip. "So total, nine hundred and thirty-three people."

What were they going to do? They were just a little ship.

"Nerissa, you listening? We're looking at possibly nine hundred and thirty-three people to get off that ship," Gabriel said. All along the ship, yellow lifeboats were bound to the side of the hull. Most of these were the new type of lifeboats: large, completely covered vessels that could hold fifty people each. Plastic and yellow, they looked like giant bathtub toys. Some of these were already in the water. Countless people were lined up on the decks, some of them climbing in. "They're loading the lifeboats."

Nerissa came back. Very likely she was watching from

a drone she had sent before her. "They'll wait until each is loaded before extending it out and dropping it into the water."

Just as she said this, one of the yellow boats lifted off the deck on a pair of mechanical arms, sweeping out over the ocean. The arms lowered it about ten feet, leaving about twenty feet of air. Then it released. Gabriel watched the lifeboat drop into the water, waves splashing all around. Then it began to move.

Just then on the other side of the ship something blew— black smoke and flame punched through the side. People swarming on the deck began to push and run as sections of the deck disintegrated. Gabriel saw two of the lifeboats topple, ripping away parts of the ship as they went. The people running, packed together, looked like dolls, far away and impossible to count or distinguish.

Misty clamped her hands over her mouth in horror at the scene.

The hair on the back of Gabriel's neck prickled as he thought of several things at once—what if there were children among them, and there had to be—how would they keep from being trampled? What were they feeling? The passengers had to be panicked. The crowd was pushing toward the fore and aft of the ship on all three decks, swarming around the loading lifeboats.

"Oh, the ship is starting to go," Cora moaned.

"Yes," Gabriel said. He heard a note of alarm enter his

voice. That wouldn't help anybody. He modulated it. "Keep your mind above it. We're here to help." Ahead of them, the *Bruno III* was listing worse than before. Now only two lifeboats remained to be loaded, with many more passengers still waiting. In the water, the yellow lifeboats were tooling away and surrounding the ship. Two of them, empties that had fallen during the explosion, lay upside down.

"Options?" Gabriel called.

"We can't take the people on," Peter said. "You'll never get them onto this ship through the hole, and they'll stampede."

"No, we need the *Nebula* for evac," Gabriel agreed.

Misty visibly set her shoulders and began counting off ideas. "We can help with the fire. And we can help people we see swimming in the water."

"I have something else," Peter said. He brought up the sonar and indicated a small shape near the ship, lighting it up separately from all the other boats moving around. "That light there? That's a lifeboat that was struck by one of the ones falling off the ship. And it's twenty feet under water and sinking."

"Are there...Are there people on it?" Gabriel asked.

Peter flipped a switch and a new screen came up on the big one, labeled UNIDIRECTIONAL MIC.

All Gabriel heard was screaming.

"DIVE," GABRIEL SAID. "Put us right over that life-boat."

"It's drifted under the cruise ship," Misty warned. "Those things are supposed to be buoyant, so if it's sinking it means they've already got a lot of water coming in. They may not have much time."

"Then we're going to have to move under the cruise ship, get between them."

"Understood," Peter said. "Diving." The sounds in the walls of the *Kekada* told them as much as the water on the viewscreen enveloped the camera and they moved down.

They moved forward and down. The huge cruise ship's shadow fell across them, and Gabriel could see it was sinking. The lifeboat was underneath it. Gabriel grimaced as they flew in through the water, moving under the hull of the cruise ship as they got closer to the lifeboat.

"Use the legs to grab either side of the lifeboat," Gabriel said. Peter hit a button and the legs started moving under them.

"Do you have anything you could float them with?" Cora pointed at the lifeboat. "To get the lifeboat up to the surface?"

Gabriel shook his head. "It's a great idea, but no." He thought. "We can use the legs to drag that lifeboat out from under the ship. But then after that...we can't *fly*, so we can only get as high as the surface; they'll still be underwater."

"Okay," Misty said smoothly. "So, Gabriel, you and me, we'll have to go outside, dive, and rescue them under the water. The passengers will be at about thirty feet. That's safe enough. How many rebreathers do we have?"

"Five," Gabriel said.

"So okay," Cora said. "I'll come, too. We'll escort five at a time. Get them to the surface, then take the rebreathers back down."

Gabriel shook his head. Cora was pretty good at planning rescues on the fly, but there was a major problem. "How do we get to them? We can't. If they're alive in there, it's an airtight boat. We open it up, it'll flood instantly." Gabriel could picture the sheer madness of water rushing in on thirty-fifty passengers in a small craft like that.

On the screen, the lifeboat was still drifting downward. He thought for a moment. "We could..."

"Bump them out from under the ship," Misty said. "That's the first thing. Otherwise it'll take them straight down when it goes."

Cora ran her fingers through her hair. "Can you get *under* the lifeboat then? Lift it up from below?"

"I don't know," Peter said. "We don't know how heavy it is, even in the water. It could crack the hull of the *Kekada*. Then we *both* sink."

"*Would* we crack? When we're pulling on weight under us with the legs, that stresses the hull," Gabriel offered. "We don't crack *then*..."

"That's how the lower hull is designed, Gabe." Peter huffed and brought up a schematic on the viewscreen, sending the camera to one corner and the sonar to another. Swiveling on the screen was a blueprint of the *Kekada*'s crablike shape, with the heavy structure underneath where the legs were housed. "Look at that. Our underhull is about three times stronger than the top. We can't hold them on top of us."

Gabriel stared at the schematic. "What if..." He turned back to run his hand down the side of his captain's chair, touching the clasp of the retracted safety harness.

"No," Misty said. "You're out of your mind."

"What if we were inverted?" Cora said, echoing his thought aloud.

"What?" Peter asked. They were nearing the lifeboat, about two hundred yards away now.

Gabriel pointed at Cora and nodded. "We invert, we just flip right over. Safety harnesses engaged. We get below them, then push up toward them, using our lower hull as the top, and push them toward the surface. You said yourself it should be strong enough."

"I didn't say that at all," Peter said. "I said it's three times stronger and also I'm not entirely certain how to control this ship upside down."

Gabriel scoffed. "You *just did it* twenty minutes ago. We're upside down when we do a loop."

"*Yeah*, and then we loop *back*."

Gabriel opened his hands. "You have any other ideas?"

"Go back in time and stock up on industrial foam that could be used to float sinking boats'd be nice," grumbled Peter.

"Everyone in their seats." Gabriel dropped into his chair, but he saw that the rest were already seated. "Misty, trigger the harnesses." Misty controlled weapons systems and had more ready access to the other automatic systems of the ship. Gabriel heard clacking through the bridge as the waist and shoulder harnesses flew into place around the whole crew. "Peter—nudge them out forty feet from beneath the cruise ship and then dive, invert, and go slow."

"Aye," Peter moaned. "Starting with the nudging."

The *Kekada* dipped toward the lifeboat, which, as it

dropped through the water, looked like a yellow submarine nearly as long as the *Kekada* was. The engines whirred as he slowed to a crawl, and there was an audible crunch as the *Kekada* collided with the lifeboat, bumping it up a little.

The lifeboat was still falling, but now the *Kekada* bumped and pushed it again. Peter caught it under the curve of the side, and the boat rose slightly in the water. The lifeboat immediately started falling again, but they were moving it out.

"Okay," Gabriel said. "We have to get away from it to turn over, so dive, fifty feet, move out sixty feet south, forty knots."

"Diving," Peter said, and the *Kekada* dropped away from the lifeboat, zooming away at nearly fifty miles an hour.

They leveled off, moving southward. On the sonar screen, the elevation of the lifeboat was falling steadily. "We should be far enough away," Gabriel said.

Cora looked back from the science station. "Have you ever been inverted in this ship?"

"Never for more than a second or two," Peter said. Peter brought the *Kekada* around and they were racing toward the lifeboat now at forty knots. "Captain?"

"Go," Gabriel said.

Peter pulled his stick to the right and they flipped, the floor of the bridge first at their side and then up above. At first Gabriel tried to hold on to the seat but quickly let go, his body falling against the safety harness. He felt the pressure against his eyes and looked over at Misty, whose hair was hanging down like a waterfall of dark curls. "How are we doing?"

"How are we doing? We are *upside down*, Gabe," Peter said through clenched teeth. He exhaled strongly. He looked green around the gills.

"Move us under them." They moved forward, the viewscreen showing the lifeboat as the *Kekada* moved toward it from below and about fifty feet away.

"Careful," Misty shouted. "We're gonna interrupt their downward momentum, we'll need to stay loose and let them take us down a few yards before we start lifting."

"So, loose, okay," Peter said. They lurched to the right and then left and were headed straight again. "I'm sorry, it's not easy to control the ship in reverse."

Gabriel's head was starting to ache already. Blood was running to his head. *No problem. Right?*

"I'm…diving the ship to go up, now," Peter said, "*sort of*—I have to use the engines as though we're diving, but blowing out the ballast tanks as though we're ascending, because we are. Air in the walls doesn't care if we're upside down."

On the screen, they were moving under the lifeboat now. It was still moving toward them and as Peter brought the center of the underside of the *Kekada* under the lifeboat, they heard a heavy *crunch* as the ships collided. All of them slapped down in their harnesses.

"Okay, we've got them," Peter rasped, sounding sick.

"Good, now move us seventy feet southward, elevating as you go."

The engines began to whine with the weight of the lifeboat. They moved slowly, the lifeboat rolling atop them. Even underwater, the hull groaned with the weight.

"Twenty feet depth," Peter said.

An alarm beeped and Misty called, "Our hull is under stress. This is not how this ship is supposed to be handled."

"They should tell us these things when they give them to us," Gabriel said.

"Fifteen feet," Peter said. "Twelve—I think the lifeboat should be coming through the surface now."

"Okay." Gabriel slapped his harness and fell toward the ceiling, flipping as he did so and landing on his feet. "Cora, Misty, let's go help them out."

Cora and Misty flipped to the ceiling and the three of them stood in the center, looking up at Peter, who was still harnessed and upside down.

They were standing next to the escape iris in the ceiling, but it was of no use to them, because to go out that way would be to flood the bridge. They headed through to the dive room, Misty jumping up a foot to slap the lock on the door. They had to climb over the transom of the door and into the dive room.

As the door shut, Gabriel climbed the shelves of the dive room to hit the flooding mechanism, and water began to pour in from above as they put on their rebreathers and goggles.

"Gabe," Peter said in his ear. "I don't know, I'm feeling woozy."

"Just take deep breaths until we've got the passengers out," Gabriel said. It was unfair, but Peter would have to stay upside down longer than they would.

The dive room was flooded, and they went out through the dive iris, up instead of down. He was so relieved when he was out in the open ocean, back oriented the way he wanted to be. He stepped onto the *Kekada*'s underhull.

Water churned all along the edge of the hull as the engines pushed to keep the *Kekada* in place. Resting right in front of them was the curved hull of the yellow lifeboat. Gabriel, Misty, and Cora swam a few feet up and their heads punched through the surface.

It was raining, three-foot waves slapping against them. Gabriel swam toward the lifeboat.

It was closed, but he could see the little window in the door on the side, where a man in a white hat was staring out at them. Gabriel grabbed a handhold on top and hauled himself up, tapping on the rain-specked glass. "Open up!"

The man inside nodded and opened the door. He was skinny, with short hair and a white officer's cap. Clearly the officer from the ship in charge of the lifeboat. Gabriel looked in.

The lifeboat was oval-shaped on the inside, lined with black benches that lay just at the line of the water that had come in. Everyone was standing on their seats. Gabriel counted thirty of them, all of them wearing yellow foam life preservers that said BRUNO CRUISE LINES.

"Who..."

"Gabriel Nemo, of the *Kekada*," he said, shaking the officer's hand. "We've stopped you sinking, but for just a moment. Does everyone have life preservers?"

"Yes," the officer said. "We're required to have one for everyone."

"Good...You have to get out."

"Out?"

"Right out onto the water," Gabriel said. "The ship under you can't hold this position long. You'll need to lead everyone out."

The man nodded, then whistled as he turned around. He shouted in Italian something Gabriel didn't understand, and the passengers all looked at one another. Then they began to follow.

Misty and Cora gathered around the door, helping people over the doorway and out onto the water. "Stick together," Cora said. "Together."

Misty took someone's hand and helped them through the door, and then called, "Peter, you still with us?"

"Still...awake," Peter's voice came. "I think it's time to talk about getting paid."

"What next?" the officer asked them as he helped someone else into the water. Waves splashed high as men and women swam.

A great horn blew, and Gabriel looked over his shoulder. Relief poured through his body.

A mountain of water was moving as the *Nebula* rose from beneath, dwarfing the cruise ship and the lifeboats that still tooled around.

"Next is ... you're going to board that," Gabriel said.

"*Nebula* to *Kekada*," Nerissa's voice came. "Is your ship *inverted*?"

"We have passengers in the water," Gabriel said. "Come after them first. Then the rest." All along the side of the *Nebula*, Gabriel saw officers springing out of hatches and dropping canisters into the water. One by one the canisters popped into shape: large, bright blue life rafts.

"Cora!" Gabriel called, and he saw her turn in the water, her body bobbing with the waves. She was next to a couple of children who didn't want to let her go. Sometimes a life preserver isn't enough. "You want to stay up with me and be helpful up here on the surface?"

"Totally," Cora called through the rain.

"Misty—why don't you go back down into *Kekada* in case Peter needs anything."

"Aye," Misty said, and she dove out of sight.

Gabriel kept helping passengers out, pointing and shouting as they swam toward the life rafts from the *Nebula*.

"Peter!"

"Captain?"

"We're clear," he said. "As soon as Misty is aboard, you're free to right yourself. Stick close."

"Copy," Peter said. Shortly Gabriel felt the water move in a great heave as the *Kekada* slipped out from underneath them.

14

BY THE TIME the *Kekada* and the *Nebula* escorted the lifeboats all the way back to the beaches at Penarth Pier, it was full evening. As the *Nebula* slipped away and the passengers swarmed on the beach, the *Kekada* rested atop the waves a quarter mile offshore.

"Let's go up top," Gabriel said. He was tired of looking through the periscope. He went to the back of the bridge and pulled down the ladder, and in a moment had the iris open. Once atop the hull, he pressed a lever in the hull with his foot. As Misty, Peter, and Cora climbed out behind him, a railing slid slowly up and clacked into place. They had a six-foot space now to lean on and look out at the ocean, or the beach, or the stars, which were just intermittently visible in the cloudy November sky.

"We're close enough to use our cell phones," Peter said. He and Misty started to make their calls while Gabriel leaned on the railing, looking out to the horizon.

Gabriel looked over his shoulder at Cora, who was staring at the land. "They'll be okay. It's better that we don't stick around. But then I guess you know that."

"I'm not looking at them," Cora said. Gabriel followed her gaze and saw she was looking at the pier. It was lit up crazily with strung lights as tourists wandered amidst jugglers and musicians.

Peter hung up and joined them, and Misty followed shortly. Now all four of them were leaning on the rail and looking to Penarth Pier as the waves lapped, occasionally splashing up to their feet.

"They're all good," Misty said. "I told them a little about what we discovered. They're relieved to know Nerissa is in shouting distance. As long as we're back by Thanksgiving."

"Well," Gabriel said, "the City hasn't asked us to stay over."

"Oh, they will," Cora said. But her voice was dreamy as she looked at the people on the pier. Gabriel heard her whisper, "What must it be like?"

"You've really never set foot on land?"

She shook her head. Gabriel understood, of course. His parents had taken a vow never to set foot on land. But he didn't get the impression that Cora was as committed to it as his parents.

"Well, you know…" Peter took off his glasses and polished them on his shirt. "I mean, you guys have amazing planters and scaly monkeys, I have to give the MIMgineers that. But do you have *candy floss?*"

"What?" she asked.

"The pink stuff." He pointed high onto the pier. He looked back at Gabriel. "What do you say, Gabe? You want to bring some back?"

"Well…" Gabriel smiled. It was a good idea.

"Oh, I couldn't," Cora said.

"Actually," Misty said. "A *pier*…isn't *land*. Not really."

"You want to see it?" Gabriel asked.

Cora stared for a long time. "Yes. Yes, I do."

Twenty minutes later, they climbed up the same ladder they had gone up two days before. "I forgot to mention," Gabriel called down to Cora as he hustled up the ladder. "We found your claw. It was how we knew you weren't Maelstrom yourselves."

"How's that?" Cora said, taking one ginger step after another. He wanted to keep talking to her, because she seemed nervous. Not for climbing sixty feet, but for what was to come.

"The inscription," Misty said. "MIM. *Mobilis in Mobili.*"

"Change in the changes." Cora nodded. The water was far below now.

Gabriel reached the top and hopped over, followed by Misty and Peter. Finally Cora popped her head up and looked around, and he and Misty gave her a hand, hauling her over.

The wide pier was teaming with people, and as the crew drew back, Cora stepped forward, her eyes wide.

A juggler across the pier dropped one of his pins and then expertly kicked it, causing it to catch fire, and he caught it again. Cora laughed and then spun in place.

They began to walk, following Cora as she moved to and fro, watching the people. Gabriel could see her eyes follow one, and then the other. She joined some children in a game of hopscotch as strands of fairy lights swayed overhead.

They finally reached the booths near the pavilion and Peter got them all cotton candy, and they drifted to the railing to look down the beach.

As Cora struggled with a bite of cotton candy, Misty showed her how to extract a chunk and fold it into a little wad. As Cora popped one in her mouth she turned to Gabriel. "So…how long did *you* go before you came to the land?"

Gabriel ignored his own cone of cotton candy after taking a little. He wasn't much on candy. "Until I was twelve. Just about eight months ago," Gabriel said. "Where did you get your interest in the land?"

She looked dreamily out to sea. "My parents were pilots. Both of them. My mother was the leader of the Watch, in fact. They…" She bit her lip. "They loved stories of the land. I was always fascinated. They both died testing a new engine, about a year ago. Nils has sort of... looked after me since then. Trained me. I just... watch the land." She looked at the candy. "And this is what *you* do." She looked at all of them. "Save people and eat candy."

He laughed. "This is what we do. Me, Misty, Peter. We use what we know to help people and, if we're lucky, help the sea."

"It *is* kind of fantastic," Peter said. "If I do say so myself."

"Let me ask you something I don't understand," Gabriel said. "You said... You do the rescues you do in secret? It's against the rules?"

"Yeah," Cora said. She looked down. "It's something we *don't* do. The highest principle is live the Nemo way. Next is protect the *Dinas*. And that means... we're secret. There's no room in there for helping. Not when it might reveal us."

Gabriel thought about how many times he had heard that. How he had been moved to keep his activity secret until recently.

"I understand," he said. "And people who feel that way can be hard to argue with. But the Nemos have chosen to risk it. My mom is now at a school near land. And Nerissa's on the run, but she helps. And we're... kind of in the open." He looked at his crew.

"I wouldn't have it any other way," Peter said. Then he

gasped a little as he stared toward the ocean. Gabriel looked where he was staring.

A pair of shadows stood still on the end of the pier.

Gabriel heard footsteps clomp down and turned. Across the pier, two more men emerged. One of them was Nils. The colors dancing on his leather jacket looked garish and inappropriate.

Nils angrily jabbed his finger toward Cora. "It's time to go."

CORA HAD SULLENLY agreed to ride back to *Dinas Nautilus* aboard the *O'Connell*. Gabriel, Misty, and Peter followed aboard the *Kekada*. Nils said that Minerva wanted to talk to them. But Gabriel had the feeling of being *in trouble*, which was not a good feeling at all.

"Well, Misty was right," Peter harrumphed as they followed the *O'Connell*. "A pier isn't land."

"I hate getting someone else into trouble," Misty said.

"That's exactly the word I was thinking," Gabriel said.

"You know when you have a friend whose parents don't let them have caffeine and you give them a Coke? It's like that," Misty continued.

They reached the City ship once more and rode the enormous elevator down into the hangar.

"Boy, that guy looked mad," Peter mumbled. "Like a mad dad."

"Like her brother," Misty said. "That's what she said she was to Nils and them, right? A little sister since her parents died?"

When they went down the ladder into the hangar, Nils and Cora were waiting for them. Cora was looking at the ground. Nils sighed and put his hands together. But he couldn't pull off the drawing-you-in kind of pose that Minerva had been so good at. "Listen. I know our rules are strange to you. So you must think I'm a monster. I promise, I'm not. The rules are there for a reason."

"It wasn't Cora's fault," Gabriel said.

Nils shook his head. "You were an enormous help with the Maelstrom. Thank you for that."

Gabriel nodded.

Nils looked at his protégé. "Cora, our guests are supposed to go talk to Minerva."

Cora asked, "Can I walk them?"

"Sure," Nils said. He kissed her head.

Cora walked them out the double doors and they made their way once again down the promenade. The clock tower said it was nearly eight o'clock, and the whole city had taken on a nighttime cast that flickered with the amber lamplights. Gabriel heard faint music piping in from some-where, an old string piece he didn't recognize.

"Do you recognize that piece?" Gabriel asked Misty and Peter.

"Not me," Peter said.

Misty shook her head. "It sounds like Vivaldi."

"It's Nils," Cora said. "He wrote it when he was about our age."

Peter pursed his lips. "What do you know? They have scaly green monkeys, and composers, too."

Cora left them at the clock tower. "I need to get back."

"Where do you stay?" Misty asked.

"At my apartment," Cora said. "Or my parents' apart-ment. It's not bad. Nils and the rest, Dr. Ramoray. They look in on me."

"We'll see ya soon," Peter said.

The door to the clock tower opened and they took the stairs past the control center up to the door that said DIRECTOR.

Gabriel shrugged, looking at the others. He knocked.

"Come in," Minerva said brightly.

As they entered, Minerva was standing with her back to them by the conference table that appeared to float. She was looking at the painting near the center of the room, though Gabriel was sure it was a different one than had been there before. Not because he remembered the last one, but because this painting was of the *Nautilus*. In the picture, the great Nemoship floated in a lagoon that Gabriel recognized right away.

"This is Lincoln Island." She looked over her shoulder, her fingers steepled in front of her. "I had this brought in just for you."

Gabriel nodded. "It's wonderful."

"Do you know it?"

"I . . . yeah. Yes, ma'am. I've been there." In fact he had been there many times, sometimes for months on end. The lagoon, protected on three sides by high cliffs, was now full of constantly evolving, modular docks and piers, and sat at the edge of a honeycomb of labs and manufacturing facilities. There were more people there now than there were at Nemolab. He had seen three ships built there. "We call it Nemobase."

"Delightful," Minerva said. "Very Nemo."

"Definitely," Peter said.

Minerva turned around and sighed. "Thank you for protecting us."

"Nils was the leader," Gabriel said. "The Watch is . . . amazing."

She tilted her head playfully, her hair swaying. "And you went to land with Cora."

Peter cleared his throat. "I mean, technically it was a . . ."

Gabriel shook his head.

". . . pier."

Minerva laughed. "That's good. I like that. Well, we all go a little off-MIM every once in a while."

Gabriel wondered about that. He was delighted by *Dinas Nautilus*, but if the City were really all about change in the changes, wouldn't that suggest that they should "go a little off" all the time? That was how changes could happen. But it seemed to mean something slightly different to Minerva. It seemed to mean drilling in more and more. Change in the sameness, more like.

She said, "It's a really busy week. Really." She shook her head with amusement. "And to tell the truth it isn't the best time to have visitors, even famous visitors, but the more I thought about it the more I realized I needed to talk to you. All three of you."

Out of nowhere, three chairs suddenly began to rise before the table and the crew stepped back. The chairs were wooden and smooth and each seemed to be all of one piece. She bade them sit.

Gabriel and Peter and Misty sat in the chairs, listening politely, as Minerva turned again, swiping her hand across the painting, and the far wall lit up, displaying the image as large as the room. She strode toward it and put her hands on the image of the *Nautilus* itself.

"I didn't know we would meet you," she said, turning around again to face them. "Gabriel, Misty, Peter. Of the *Obscure*, and now the *Kekada*. Although I'm not sure why that happened."

"Blew up," Peter said.

She pointed. "We missed that. But we were aware that you were active. Out there. Discovering. Living the Nemo life. I dare say a MIM life."

Gabriel said, "Thank you, but how? How did you know?"

She shrugged. "If you're going to hide on the bottom of the ocean, you need to get reports of the world. We have drones. Satellites. Hackers. We keep busy. But we had no idea you would ever stand here in the City." She cleared her throat, a little beat to indicate she was going to shift the subject. "We have a great moment coming up. Something that I would be so delighted if you would be a part of."

Misty asked, "What's that?"

"Tomorrow," Minerva said, "is the Day of Dakkar." She turned, producing the silver controller and clicking it. The image of Nemo at Lincoln Island disappeared, replaced with a different painting of Nemo. Here, he stood in his full princely dress, years earlier than before, on a beach. He bore a sword, which hung down in his hand. His other arm was in a cast.

"It is the day that, one hundred and fifty years ago, Prince Dakkar gave up his kingdom and his name. The rebellion he joined against the British Empire had failed. His family had been slaughtered. And on that day, Prince Dakkar turned his back on the land and declared himself monarch of the seas. He took his intelligence and knowledge of science, engineering, and the sea, and he gave up his name. And he became Nemo."

Gabriel's heart swelled. All this he had heard before, but few were as poetic as Minerva. He had no idea if she had the date right. But the story was true.

Misty said, "Did you say tomorrow?"

"We are a planning an event larger than we have ever undertaken. It will occupy the attention of the entire city. And it would do me such great honor if you three would be a part of it. We want you to be here as part of the Nemo legacy." She opened her hands. "Will you join us for our Destiny Day event?"

Gabriel looked at the others.

"*Thursday?*" Misty whispered.

"Dude," Peter said. "Yeah, that's..."

"That sounds amazing," Gabriel said. "I mean, I don't know what all it is."

"Hey!" Peter said. "We gotta talk about this."

Gabriel nodded. Sure, they'd talk about it. Parents and all that. He smiled. "I guess we gotta talk about it. Can we..."

"Certainly, you can talk about it," Minerva said. "But the invitation is open. You'd be honored guests. And for that matter, I expect you to be our guests tonight."

"That, yeah..." Misty nodded toward Minerva and then back at Gabriel. "That we can do. Can we..." She gestured with her head toward the door.

"We're gonna talk," Gabriel said. Misty was already rising, her face burning.

"Of course," Minerva said with her usual brightness. "That's the team spirit. You can let me know in the morning."

They thanked her and moved out. Misty was silent as she led them down the stairs, but her tromping on the promenade said a lot.

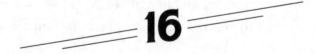

16

MISTY STOOD OUTSIDE the clock tower and scanned the promenade intently.

"What are you looking for?" Gabriel asked.

"I'm just looking for a good place to talk."

"Check that out," Peter said, pointing to a gazebo in the distance, opposite the direction of the hangar. The gazebo's pointy top was of shiny, speckled metal, and appeared to be the head of an octopus, with the arms reaching down to form the columns of the gazebo. He started walking toward it, and they followed him under fruit trees and amber lights until they reached it.

When they reached the gazebo, they walked up coral steps into it. Gabriel saw a brass plaque on the column closest to him. It said the gazebo had been built twenty years after the founding of the City. On the Day of Dakkar. Gabriel wondered who had been director then.

Misty strode across the gazebo and stopped and turned back to Gabriel with her arms folded. She looked down and shook her head, scoffing. "We . . . *can't* stay for this."

"We actually don't even really know what this is," Peter observed.

"I mean, it's an event." Gabriel shrugged. "We know that much. It seems to be very important to them—how amazing is it that we would find this society, and get a chance to observe their celebration of their memories . . ."

Misty said, "Oh, I get it: the memories of Nemo. In fact I get that this is very much attached to *you*. But Gabriel: We're supposed to be back for Thanksgiving."

Gabriel shook his head. Surely, she could see this was bigger than that. "Yeah. No, I get that."

"*Do* you?"

"I know we have a deadline to . . . it's turkey."

"It's *not*," she said, wringing her hands, "just a deadline. Gabriel, this is important to my family, and Peter's family . . . it's important to *me*."

Gabriel understood family traditions. He had plenty. But a meal couldn't possibly be worth missing an event the world of land had never seen before.

Peter said to Misty, "Hey. Tell him about it. There's no way he would know."

Misty rubbed her jaw and looked up at the ceiling of

the gazebo, which had a single bright copper sun that bore a swirling MIM in the center.

"Okay. When my parents were deployed they would be gone, one or the other, for eight months at a time. Sometimes more. But being home for Thanksgiving was something that they said they would do *anything* for so that they would be able to come back and sit down and have a Thanksgiving feast with me and my sister." She was looking out on the promenade now, lost in the memory. She scoffed. "Sometimes a month before, I would start to ask myself, *What if my mom doesn't remember what I look like?* And yeah, we had Skype, so of course they really knew, but it was like, what if they don't remember what I *am*. From moment to moment. And Thanksgiving was when we would be able to reconnect."

She turned back to Gabriel, wiping her face with the back of her hand as she sniffed. "It is *so* important to me. And hearing you think that maybe we can just...*skip* it." She shook her head.

Gabriel thought about the time he'd spent with his own family under the ocean. In those days, it was usually just him and his parents and the people who worked at Nemolab, and he was with them every day. No one in his family had been gone for any extended period of time until his sister had finally left with the *Nebula*. Now his father *was* far away under the ocean. But since coming to California, he had learned what it was to miss family.

He had been so caught up in the fact that these people were connected to his family. They looked up to the name of Nemo, and that was so cool and new and refreshing to him. But he had to be honest: There was no way it would mean the same thing to Misty and Peter.

Gabriel turned to Peter. "Do you feel the same way?"

Peter shrugged. "Well, my mom was never deployed, but I know what she's talking about... *aaannd* yes."

Gabriel leaned on an octopus column. He thought about priorities.

"Okay. I have to admit, I want to know everything about these people. Hearing them talk about how they've taken these ideas that I live by and turned them into a whole society, that's something I could listen to, day in and day out. But... they're not you guys."

They just stared. Misty sniffed again.

"If what's important to you is that we're back tomorrow morning to be with your families... then that's what's most important to me." He stepped up and put his hands on their shoulders. "Don't even think about it anymore. We stay tonight, and then we'll go home."

Peter and Misty looked at each other. Misty smiled.

"Works for me," Peter said.

17

CORA CALLED OUT, "Guys!" and came running up to stop by the steps of the gazebo. "I was looking for you."

Gabriel waved. "We're just enjoying your gazebo."

"Well, you have a visitor."

They followed her to the hangar. This time Cora led them through another door to the side of the big entrance, and they emerged in the hangar's control room. One officer was at a chair next to the elevator controls. The hangar was filled with water already.

Cora pointed up. "A ship is lowering." Indeed, one of the elevators was coming down. Then she looked at the others. "I'm really glad you decided to stay. I don't know where your rooms are, though."

"Cool," Misty said. She seemed to be feeling better

now that they had settled Thursday, and Gabriel felt relieved himself.

Peter looked at the elevator. "It's not a ship."

On the elevator sat a silvery vehicle with large, rugged wheels: a Nemorover. Gabriel knew that it had to have been lowered from the *Nebula* by powerful cables into place atop *Dinas Nautilus*.

The visitor was Nerissa.

Nils entered the control room. "So we're getting a visit from more than one Nemo," he said. "Amazing." He looked at Gabriel. "You should be glad we recognized the *Nebula* or there would have been another general alarm."

As soon as the elevator stopped, Nerissa didn't wait for the hangar to drain. He could see through her windshield that she was wearing a pressure suit already, so she popped the rear hatch of the Nemorover and swam out. She moved expertly in the suit, whipping like a dolphin toward the control room of the hangar. By the time the place had drained, she was already standing at the door at the top of the stairs inside the hangar, unlatching her helmet and knocking on the door.

One of the control room crew opened the door and Nerissa stayed outside it, casting her eyes only at Nils. "Nerissa Nemo. Asking permission to come aboard."

"Nils Ramoray. Permission granted," Nils said. He smiled and shook her hand.

Nils led them out onto the promenade and Gabriel kept

his eyes on his sister, trying to gauge her reaction as they walked under fruit trees and lamplights. Here and there, citizens sat in the grass, occasionally looking their way.

"What made you decide to come?" Gabriel asked.

"I wanted to see what this city of *Nautilus* was all about." She looked around, wide-eyed, but he couldn't tell what she was thinking.

They reached the tower and Nerissa asked if she could see the control room, but Nils stopped her. "We're still recalibrating things after having to make our sudden move. You understand."

"Of course."

Cora looked up at the clock. It was 9:15 P.M. She gasped. "Did you guys even eat?"

The crew looked at one another. Nerissa said, "No, we've been busy on the *Nebula*."

"I hadn't thought about it," Gabriel said.

"Cotton candy," Peter said. "That's it."

"There's a café near the auditorium at the fore of the promenade," Nils said, indicating the direction of the gazebo. "I can't join you, but they can make anything you like."

"Is it all seaweed?" Peter asked. "Don't answer that. I'm used to it."

Nils laughed. Then he said to Nerissa, "Now if you'll excuse me, I have to attend to the work of the Watch. But you're in good hands with Cora." He turned to the *Kekada* crew. "Gabriel and crew, we've assigned you rooms. I'll have the café staff let Cora know where your rooms are, and she can direct you." He shook Nerissa's hand and bowed slightly, then disappeared through the door of the clock tower.

They walked past the tower and the gazebo, following the brook with its fish. Nerissa listened for a moment.

"Vivaldi?"

"Nils, actually," Gabriel said.

"No kidding."

"Brilliant family—we met his mom. She's the local genetic engineering genius."

After walking a long way, Gabriel heard a piano and saw a staircase with wrought-iron railings and ivy covering it. Cora stopped in front of it. "I actually don't eat here often. There's a general hall for meals. But it's nice for a treat."

"Perfect," Nerissa said. "Hey, Peter, Misty—if you guys could find us a table, I wanted to chat with Gabriel?"

Cora, Misty, and Peter nodded. "No problem," Cora said. "We'll find a spot and I'll figure out where your rooms are."

Then they were alone on the promenade by the stairs. Gabriel listened to the piano and felt the gentle, weird thrum of the engines far below his feet. "So?"

Nerissa rubbed her jaw and took it all in. The lamps. The balconies. The tower. The brass. "I mean . . . I think it's a Victorian nightmare. Except for the frilly collars. That's just strange."

Gabriel knew what she meant. "I don't know. It's like they're a city out of time. But you know, my library looked like this. Kind of."

"Sure, I get it," Nerissa said. "But you made the *library* look like that, not your whole life. These guys are different. They don't have another life." Gabriel thought about the inside of the *Nebula*, which was as far from Victorian as you could get; it was all swooping metal and white surfaces. She was the closest in his family to carrying on the Nemo tradition, but for her, *Mobilis in Mobili* had meant leaving the world of brass and wood far behind.

"I wonder what the rooms are like?" he mused.

"See for yourself." Nerissa put her hand on Gabriel's shoulder. "Anyway. Time moves forward for a reason."

They went into the café and a waiter in armbands led them to a table in the back. "Gabriel!" Cora said. She indicated a place for him and Nerissa to sit. "I got your rooms. You and Peter will share, and Misty will be with me. I'm so excited." She laughed. "I *never* have guests."

Misty clinked glasses with Cora. "Me, neither."

The table was white with brass settings, and featured a brass candlestick with a glowing orb on top. A basket held bread that, when Gabriel sampled it, tasted like bread with just a slight texture to tell him it was, in fact, seaweed.

Cora ordered for them and seemed thrilled to do it, and soon the table was overflowing with pasta made of seaweed, and octopus for Peter, and shark steak for Misty and Nerissa.

"What do you make the butter from?" Nerissa asked as she buttered a roll. "It's impressive." That was high praise from her.

"Whale milk and fish oil," Cora said, clasping her hands.

It was all fantastic. "So," Peter said, "now that we got you in trouble, what else can we tell you about the outside world?"

A painful sort of wave passed over Cora's face when Peter mentioned her being in trouble. Gabriel saw Peter register that his humor hadn't landed the way he wanted to. But Cora recovered quickly, sidestepping and turning toward Gabriel's sister. "What I want to know is about the *Nebula*. Let's start with ... What was the first thing you did when you launched that amazing ship?"

Nerissa laughed. "I can't believe you'd want to hear about it."

"Oh, come on," Cora said. "Anyone who goes around in a submarine trying to help the sea wants to hear about how you got your start."

Nerissa shook her head, sipped some water, and said, "Okay."

The tale of the *Nebula*'s first adventure took up nearly half an hour. Gabriel had never heard her talk so much, and it made his heart swell.

When they were done, they reached the stairway in front of the café and a pair of men in leather jackets—Gabriel thought they might be Minerva's staff, but they carried batons on their waists, so they might be guards—arrived.

"Captain Nemo," one of the guards—for that was how Gabriel had decided to think of them—looked at Nerissa. "We're here to escort you back to your vehicle."

Nerissa began to go with the guards, who arranged themselves in front of her but didn't start walking until she did. She looked back. "Gabriel? We'll be in the area."

Gabriel watched her go as Cora led them off the main path. The door into the dwellings—Cora's area—was polished wood, with a dragon door knocker. The number above the knocker said 13.

Cora unlocked the door with a swipe of her palm, and they entered a foyer awash in golden tile and bric-a-brac, from little columns on which sat small paintings and photos to countless framed portraits on the wall. Beyond the foyer was a gorgeous, wide, dark wooden staircase. They began to climb.

"We're on the seventh floor," Cora said.

"No elevator?" Peter said.

"The only elevator here is in the clock tower," Cora said.

Cora said good night to Gabriel and Peter at their door.

"We're down the hall," she said. Then she and Misty waved, and Peter shut the door.

Peter said, "Well, this is nice."

The rooms were as overdecorated and strangely old-fashioned as the foyer. As Peter ran in and flopped on a Victorian love seat, gilded lamps turned on, casting a yellowish glow about the room. A fake fireplace ignited under a pink coral mantel on which sat an array of domed clocks, statues, and cameos. Someone had left them a pitcher of water between a pair of enormous canopy beds. It was all so Nemo.

Gabriel went to a pair of French doors and threw them open. Outside were the trees of the promenade with the music filtering in. And a scent, something like honeysuckle. "You could almost forget you were at the bottom of the ocean. And I say that as someone who was *born* at the bottom of the ocean."

Peter joined him on the balcony, but not before stopping at a bowl of fruit and grabbing an apple. He took a bite, swallowed, then yawned. "I just realized something."

"What's that?"

"We've been at it for two days now." He shook his head. "I gotta get some sleep."

"Me, too," Gabriel said.

They shut the balcony and climbed into the enormous beds. The covers were knitted imitation cotton, probably made from hammered seaweed as well. Through the sheer curtains over the French doors, Gabriel could see the vague outline of the curlicue-shaped bars of the balcony.

It wasn't a Victorian nightmare, as Nerissa had said. No, not at all. It was like a World of Nemo. He was sorry he was going to miss the event.

Smiling, Gabriel drifted off to sleep.

18

GABRIEL AWOKE IN the middle of the night to a couple of sounds. Only one was obvious at first: the distant chiming of the great clock in the tower in the center of the promenade. The other he couldn't remember now that he'd awoken. All he heard besides the dying chime was the steady breathing of Peter. They shared a room all the time, so this was just the normal sound of night for him.

He lay awake and let his eyes adjust to the light. The room slowly came into view: the canopy over the bed with its ghostly white cloth, the white doilies on the wooden table, the shining of the legs of the table itself.

Clack.

Gabriel sat up, touching the silver lamp next to him,

and an artificial flame lit atop it, just like a bedside candle in an old book. "Peter."

"Whuh?" Peter turned over, lifting his head. "Whazzit."

Clack.

Gabriel took the candlestick in hand and walked through the room to the French doors at the end, looking out through the curtains to the promenade below. He could see clear across to the darkened balconies and rooms of countless citizens of *Dinas*. The latch for the balcony was silver and curlicued like everything else, and it slid open easily.

Stepping onto the balcony was like stepping out into the night overlooking a park from two hundred years ago. He could see no one on the promenade below. The great clock gave off its glow, setting the trees and the babbling brooks in shadow.

He leaned over, peering far down the promenade. He couldn't see much past the central tower, so the far-off doors to the hangar where the *Kekada* lay were invisible. To his right, he could see the staircases at the end of the promenade, leading up to large doors that had to go to more official rooms, more theaters and dining halls, or so Cora had told them.

His foot brushed something, and he looked down to see three small stones.

Peter, now standing, said, "What is it?"

Gabriel caught movement to his left and spun, swatting away another pebble with the candlestick as it lobbed toward the balcony. Standing on a balcony about twelve feet away were Misty and Cora.

"What are you doing?" Gabriel whispered to them.

"Getting your attention," Cora said.

"You couldn't call me on the wristband?"

Misty shook her head. "They can probably listen to the wristbands."

Peter looked out and joined him on the balcony. He shook his head when he looked across to the other balcony, muttering, "What, what, what..."

"What's going on?" Gabriel asked. "You can't sleep?"

"The beds are nice," Peter whispered.

"*Everything's* nice," Misty said. "It's like sleeping in *A Christmas Carol*. But no, Cora wanted us all up."

Gabriel glanced at Cora, who looked ill in the light of her imitation candlestick.

She said, "I have something to show you."

"Okay, let's meet in the hall." He gestured with his head.

"No, we'll be seen." Cora gestured downward. "We have to go this way, down the balconies."

Gabriel looked down and back at Peter. "What do you think?"

Peter handed Gabriel his boots. "I think you shouldn't do it barefoot."

The balconies had twisted iron railings done up in countless flower designs, and it was easy to grab on to them and lower his body until his toes were almost touching the balcony below. Gabriel looked over and Misty was in the same position. He whispered, "What do you think?"

"Drop and grab it as you go."

"On the count of three," Gabriel said. He counted, and then dropped, the next balcony flying up toward him, and caught it, his feet sliding to a stop on the outside of the railing. Shimmied down. Misty counted this time, hanging in the air next to him. Drop. Grab. Shimmy. And again.

They reached the third floor and Gabriel called up, "Okay."

Peter nodded and gave a pretty decent approximation of Gabriel's performance. He slid over the balcony and clung to the outside of the railing.

Gabriel reached the second floor. The balcony before him was lit up, but the curtains were drawn. He slid down to the bottom of the railing and looked down. The next stop was the grass of the promenade, next to the walkway. He swung, dropping, and hit the grass rolling. Misty landed next to him.

A moment later Cora and Peter rolled after them.

Misty wiped her hands against each other and shrugged at Cora. "Okay."

"This way," Cora said. She led them along the grass. They stayed off the path, because that was where most of the light was. They moved quickly and silently until they reached a pair of silver doors near the end of the promenade, not far from the café.

"What is this?" Gabriel asked.

Cora said, "It's the way to Oceanics." Just then the doors began to open inward, and they heard voices.

The four of them scattered to the side, pressing themselves against the wall as two people stepped out, talking amongst themselves. One of them, towering over the other, was Minerva. She was annoyed. "How could we be low on feed already?" she asked. "We're supposed to be generating enough every day..."

"I'm sorry," the man with her said. "But we had to take the generators offline when we moved north. We should be caught up in a day"

"Let's be caught up in half a day," Minerva told him, putting her hand on his shoulder, and as they drifted from earshot Gabriel heard her say, "Wouldn't that be more Nemo?"

The doors were still open. Cora nodded to the others and the four darted through the doors even as they started to close.

The room inside was dark. "She was up late," Gabriel said.

Cora led them on. "Busy lady." They walked on and a door at the end of the room opened automatically. They were in a silvery hall now, which reminded Gabriel of the inside of the *Nebula*. Metal. Easy to clean. They passed several doors, one labeled KITCHEN. Then past long glass windows showing dimly lit gardens. Automatic sprinklers moved along the ceiling inside, spraying water in the dark.

Gabriel had the distinct feeling of being backstage.

They got to the end of the hall and turned, and Cora stopped at another door that said simply OCEANICS.

It opened automatically, and the four stepped into a hallway that lit itself. The door shut behind them. Along the corridor were long windows, with lights flickering and dancing in the corridor. They were full of water and movement.

"Oh," Misty said, pointing to a plaque next to one of the tanks. "This one is food fish. Oh, and here are the cephalopods."

"Yes," Cora said. "We actually have to farm a lot of seafood because it can be difficult to predict what we can catch." That made sense. There were thousands of people in the City. The feeding of them couldn't be left to chance. "Especially," she added, "now that the sea is so polluted."

They looked through the window to see a habitat of wood and plants, more or less re-creating the ocean floor. He saw two or three octopuses, but couldn't see the back of the tank, so there could be hundreds. The window into the tank was thirty feet long. They moved down, taking several seconds to pass by each window, because the tanks were enormous.

Sharks. Barracuda. Octopuses. Squid. Countless small food fish. At the end, the tank windows on either side stopped at a silver frame that extended to a silver panel covering the top half of the wall at the end of the corridor.

"Now," Cora said, "you met Dr. Ramoray. She's retired. But you remember Ricou and how he's different, right?"

She stepped into the middle of the hall.

"Yes. Of course."

"She didn't *want* to retire. Gabriel, she can do anything. If there's a system on this ship, she probably either built it or can change it. But there were things she didn't want to do anymore. And she only told me about it recently."

Something bumped behind Cora, making the silver of the wall vibrate. She turned to the wall, and Gabriel saw it was actually a wide, closed panel. It bumped again, the metal paneling of the lower half of the wall vibrating.

Along the seam between the silver panel, Gabriel saw a long, smooth indentation about the width of a thumb, with an inset button of silver.

Cora touched the button. The silver panel flew up.

Now they looked through a panel of glass into a tank many times taller and deeper than the others.

Light danced in the corridor as they gasped and stepped back. Something bumped against the glass. A sizzling tentacle burned in the water and swiped past them. A head the shape of a giant crawdad swung by and then swam on, the creature's body undulating and swimming back, joined by three or four more.

The tank was so vast that there were shipwrecks in it, and Gabriel thought dizzily of the fake wrecks in the bottom of fish tanks. Some of the creatures wore the shells of old boats, as well.

"Lodgers," Gabriel said. "You're keeping Lodgers."

"It's not just that," Cora said. "We *made* the Lodgers—"

"What, that's crazy," Peter interrupted.

"They were supposed to clean up the pollution," Cora explained.

Gabriel's head swam. "But they're way over in the Pacific, they evolved from the petroleum-eating creatures at the bottom and ..." *And ate plastic in the ocean*, he thought.

"That was where they were needed," Cora said. "Anyway, it didn't work. Because somebody stopped them."

Misty's eyes grew wide. "*We* stopped them."

"Now," Cora said. "Look at this."

She stepped a few feet down and across the hall and hit a button. Another panel flew up.

Gabriel tore his eyes away from the Lodgers in the tank, still rocked by what Cora had said. Inside the next tank was a shipwrecked boat that had to be sixty feet away.

Slowly curling its way out of the shipwreck was a giant snake. Then another. And another.

"Kaa wasn't a one-off," Gabriel whispered.

"No," Cora said. "He was a first attempt that got away."

The giant snakes swooped past the tank, lights flashing on their little metal boxes as giant teeth snapped.

Gabriel stepped back. "You've made...a nest of sea serpents."

19

"WE NEED TO talk," Gabriel said. His head was swimming, like someone had grabbed the metal hallway and spun it around him. He closed his eyes and opened them, looking at Cora. "But we can't do it here."

He wasn't following anymore. He was leading. He began walking and pushed straight out to the hallway and then to the promenade, stopping to look up and down, before springing off his left foot to sprint toward the octopus gazebo.

The brass plaque again. Everything built around the Day of Dakkar. MIM. He stood in the center of the gazebo as Misty, Peter, and Cora came up behind him.

Cora opened her mouth to say something, but he cut her off. "Why did you show this to us?" He turned around. Her eyes were pleading.

"I knew you had to see it," she said.

"But why?" Gabriel asked. He looked at Misty, who had put her hand on Cora's shoulder because the girl was trembling. "We already knew you made a big snake that got away. So you have a tank full of them. And a tank full of Lodgers. Who you say you made to clean up pollution."

"Yeah," Peter said. "I find that one really hard to believe. Those things evolved to eat the Great Pacific Garbage Patch."

The giant Lodgers had appeared over the Patch and frightened everyone from the shipping industry to the US and Chinese navies. But the crew had assumed them to be natural.

Cora shook her head. Her voice was husky. "No, because that would have taken millions of years of evolution. And the ocean doesn't *have* millions of years. The coral reefs don't even have decades before they're dead with the way the water is warming. Antarctica is getting warmer than New York. The ocean is *dying*. And it all comes back to what those people do to it." She pointed up. Out of the City. Into the dryland world.

Gabriel felt like he'd been slapped, and he'd just gotten to the dryland world. He definitely felt like his friends had been assaulted. And yet everything he wanted to say sounded small. Defenseless. They were picking up starfish on the beach and throwing them back, but there were millions of starfish on the beach. He understood why someone from the City of Nautilus would be so angry with them.

That explained everyone else.

It didn't explain Cora.

"If you're so angry with the drylanders...why did you show us this?"

She said, "Because they're just...people. Doing the things they do. Walking on land that I'm not allowed to walk on, and do you think even one of them wakes up every day and says, because of the choices my world is making I'm going to destroy the ocean? They don't *know*, they're innocent, we can't just..." Tears were in her eyes. *"I watch them."*

Of course. Because in her world, to *watch* was to protect.

"You can't just *what*?" Peter asked, picking up on something Gabriel had heard.

Gabriel was hearing Minerva's words. *Wouldn't that be more Nemo? What does this planter want?*

What does this little worm that eats petroleum want? Can we make it more Nemo?

If we wanted to make the world more Nemo, what would the world want? What would we do with the people who are causing the problems?

What was more Nemo *now*?

We would be so honored if you would be part of this event.

"What is the Destiny Day event?" he asked.

"I don't know," she said.

"Really? Because you woke us up in the middle of the night to show us those tanks . . . You must know something." Gabriel paused. Cora seemed distraught, and he felt like he was only making it worse.

Like maybe he'd been making everything worse. Like stopping the Lodgers from coming to the surface had helped in one way but had stopped the City's plan to have them eat the pollution. Everywhere he turned he tried to make things better—what if he always made it worse? But now the City had moved onto something else. A Plan B. And he needed to know. "We can't just . . . *what?*" he repeated.

"I just know it's big," Cora insisted. "And the City will be watching, and a lot of people will be deployed. But I don't know what it is."

"Where?" Misty asked.

"I don't know, but I'd have to guess it'll be around here."

The crew glanced at one another. Misty's and Peter's families were around here. In Cardiff.

He looked down, thinking back to Minerva's office. "There was a door next to Minerva's lift. It said DESTINY." Gabriel looked up. "I'll bet the answers are in there."

They made their way down the dark promenade, leaping over the brook in several places. So quiet that Gabriel could hear the bleating of insects in the trees.

They reached the clock tower and Gabriel went to the door. It didn't open.

But it did for Cora. It either wasn't locked for citizens, or Cora was well-known enough, or enough of a member of the Watch, that it opened for her. Through the little entry foyer Gabriel saw a smaller group of officers than had been there in the day. It was noisy in there. All kinds of talking. One of the officers started to turn—maybe from the sound of the door, although Gabriel doubted it—but by that time they had already ducked into the stairwell. Up.

When they reached the landing with the door marked DIRECTOR, Gabriel stopped them all. "If she's in there . . . we drop this. We don't talk. We run to the hangar. Cora"—he put his hand on her arm, lightly—"thank you, really. I understand what you've risked. As soon as you have the door open, I think you should hurry back to Dr. Ramoray's. If we're gonna get caught you don't want to be anywhere nearby."

Cora looked at Misty and Peter and wrinkled her nose. "Does he always give that speech?"

They spoke over one another. "Always." "All the time."

She touched the door. Gabriel held his breath as it swung open.

Minerva was not there. Apparently, even the busiest lady goes home eventually. They stepped inside. Same floating conference table, without the magic chairs. Gabriel led them to the back corner, next to the lift and the big wall where a few hours ago he had seen a big painting of his ancestor.

The door marked DESTINY slid open as they neared it.

They walked into a darkened room with a great screen and a couple of workstations. Also a jelly-clear section of a wall where someone had been writing, like on a whiteboard.

6 S

1 P

2 L

3 M

"6S, 1P, 2L, 3M," Peter read aloud. To Cora he said, "Anything?"

"No idea."

Misty dropped down to a curved chair behind one of the workstations facing the screen. As she did so, the screen lit up. Music started to play.

Gabriel and the other two looked over her shoulder. On the little screen in front of Misty, a brass oval floated with the words PLAY SIMULATION.

Simulation? Gabriel nodded. "Let's do it." Misty tapped the oval.

The big screen suddenly lit up. They were looking down on a map. A blue swath of ocean protruded north from the Atlantic from the southern British coast.

"That's Bristol Channel."

From the bottom of the screen, six silvery shapes began

to move. Cora swiped her hands in the air and zoomed in. The 3D graphic was nearly perfect. They were the snakes, undulating toward the shore.

She zoomed back out as one of the snakes broke off. A red flashing target, a bull's-eye, showed over a part of the shore.

A word flashed across the screen. PIER. Cora gasped. It was her favorite place to watch.

Two more snakes were moving toward a spot farther up. The perfect graphics showed the dam across Bristol Channel. "There're the locks of the barrage, the dam," Gabriel said. One of the snakes was headed for each of two locks, or entryways, along the dam. A target appeared. LOCKS.

On the other side of the dam, the channel swarmed with computer simulations of sailboats and pleasure cruises. Three more of the snakes were already over the dam and a target lit up over the hundreds of tiny dots of activity on the other side of the water.

MERMAID QUAY.

Running along the side of the screen was a clock. It read: 7:50. The minutes ticked by in seconds.

And then, impact: A snake's head hit the pier. Two more hit the locks of the dam. Three more hit the quay. Three targets pulsated red.

10:00.

DESTINY.

The image froze.

Gabriel had to take a step back. They were going to use the snakes to attack Cardiff Bay and Penarth Pier. Six of them, simultaneously. "6S, 1P, 2L, 3M."

Misty nodded. "Six … serpents. Total. One for the pier. Two for the locks. Three to attack Mermaid Quay."

"There's gonna be…" Gabriel tried to picture it. Countless people. Cotton candy. Ice-skating on the quay. Sailboats in the path. Countless. Snakes chewing on the locks. Probably breaking them apart. "It'll be mayhem."

Cora was reading inside her goggles. "Um. It says, do you want to run again?"

"No," Gabriel said. "No, that's enough."

"There's something else," she said, jerking her head. "It says MESSAGE TO THE DRYLANDERS."

"What is it?" Gabriel asked. Cora tapped the air and he could envision an envelope opening, though really, he had no idea what she was saying.

"There's directions," she said. "It says, '*Minerva reads before camera*' and then there's a lot of notes: '*Be firm, be calm, project authority…*' then some wardrobe stuff."

"What's the message?" Gabriel said. He shouldn't even wait for it. They should be running already. But if he was going to warn the world, he needed to know all he could.

"'*This is our message to the leaders of the citizens of dry land,*'" Cora read. "'*We are going to protect the ocean. Signal your assent to our coming instructions, or what we have demonstrated in Cardiff Bay will occur again. We will repeat this demonstration daily.*

*Around the world. Until you signal your assent. When you assent,
we will show you how to be more ... Nemo.'"*

"No!" Gabriel wanted to throw up. They were going to
destroy a seaport and then threaten to terrorize the entire
sea ... and use his name to do it. And Minerva probably
thought that was exactly what Captain Nemo would have
wanted. That the oceans would be saved when the drylanders were frightened into submission. And the nauseating part was that she probably thought it was what Gabriel
would want. Because didn't he want to make the world *more
Nemo?* "No, no, no."

Cora pushed up her goggles. "What do you want to do?"

"I know one thing," Misty said, pulling out her phone
and clicking a picture of the plan.

Gabriel shook his head. Options? He knew the options.

"We need out of this City and we need to stop this
plan." He was staring at the simulation. He brought his earpiece out of his pocket and put it in his ear as he gestured
toward Cora. "And you ... I think you need to get safe."

"But ...," Cora said.

"We have to go," Gabriel said. Misty and Peter started
to move. Cora followed. Gabriel's mind was already laying
out their path: promenade, hangar, how to flood the hangar.
Someone had to be in the control booth. What if there was
already someone in the control booth? What would they
do then?

And he needed to call Nerissa. He thumbed a button and whispered into the earpiece, *"Nebula?"*

On the earpiece, Nerissa crackled on. "This is *Nebula*, what's happening?"

"We're making a run for it," Peter said. "The *Dinas* guys are . . . crazy."

"This is news?" Nerissa asked.

Gabriel shook his head as they hurried. They had to sneak past the control room. "Hang on, we have to do some sneaking."

They came down to the last set of stairs. Out to the foyer.

They snuck past the control room without a sound, and out the door.

But that was the end of the line.

Because standing there were Minerva, Nils, and four of the Watch, two on each side.

20

"CAPTAIN NEMO," MINERVA said. No leaning forward. No hands clasped together. Firm. Authoritative. "Is there something we can help you with?"

Gabriel watched her, watched her eyes. He had no idea what was real about her. Could she really believe this stuff, that he would join them in trying to take over the earth? Really? "Yeah," he said coolly. Misty and Peter fanned out slowly next to him, one on either side. Cora stepped in beside Peter. "You can help me by telling me the presentation showing a bunch of snakes eating Wales is just some special new kind of video game."

"Oh, no," she said, frowning. "We don't think it'll be entertaining at all. We're not doing it because we want to.

We're doing it because the earth *wants* it. *Needs* it. It needs more...Nemo."

"Stop! Saying that!" he fumed, his fists balled.

"Did *you* know about this?" Cora lashed out at Nils. "Did you know what they were planning?"

Nils shook his head. "I can see that you're not ready to understand."

"I understand *plenty*," Cora said. "But it's *wrong*. Do you think my parents would have gone along with it? Would your *mother*?"

"Dr. Ramoray isn't relevant to our plans going forward," Minerva said evenly.

A voice crackled in Gabriel's earpiece. "His mother would not," came an elderly female voice. "Gabriel, Peter, Misty? Listen to me."

"Nils," Cora pleaded. "She doesn't have to be the director! This doesn't have to be our *plan*. We can stop this right now. The people gathered for the Destiny Day festivities will never know what you were about to do. You can arrest her right now."

Nils sighed. "Cora. That's not gonna happen."

"I have access to the hangar controls," Dr. Ramoray said in Gabriel's ear. "But I won't be able to hold them for long. Look for the opportunity to run."

"It's time to go. All of you," Nils said. Two members of the Watch drew batons from their waists and flicked them, and they began to flare.

Gabriel bent to whisper to Cora, "Are you coming?" It was a sudden decision, but he had no doubt about it. Although he had no actual idea what she would say.

She straightened her shoulders. Nodded. So that was that.

"Look," Nils said. "I don't expect you to understand. But Minerva hasn't steered us wrong. That has to be true now."

Cora looked horrified. She said sadly, "I believe you believe that."

"Cora, you need to go back to your—"

Something chittered above them in the dark. Gabriel and Misty and Peter were expecting it. The guards weren't.

A scaly green monkey cried out and landed in the hair of the farthest guard on the right, who flailed and screamed.

Misty leapt like a panther, twisting sideways and rolling her shoulders against the lower legs of the guard on the far left. Gabriel went for the next one on Nil's right. Peter and Cora took the opposite side. Hitting low. The Watch men crumpled in surprise, their batons rolling out of their hands.

Nils and Minerva stared in shock, but Nils recovered more quickly, lunging for Gabriel. But by then they were moving.

With the guards shouting and Ricou chittering behind them, the crew ran for the hangar.

21

THE NEMOGRIP SOLES of Gabriel's boots dug into the grass as the crew headed down the promenade, leaping over a stream where golden trout shimmered in the dim light. The guards were coming, shouting behind them. There was nowhere to lose them—their only option was to make it to the hangar doors first.

The City's old-fashioned alarm bells erupted, and along the promenade, in story after story of personal rooms, lights came on as they ran. Gabriel saw children and adults coming out on their balconies. Shouting.

"I coulda told you those guys were up to no good," Peter said.

"We're up to good," Cora said. "But hurting people is going too far."

A guard in a leather jacket came running out from the side and Gabriel ducked under his flaring baton. Misty moved expertly, grabbing the guard by the forearm and spinning, sending the guard tripping in the direction he had been going. They heard the splash and a cacophony of quacking as the guard went sprawling into a duck pond.

"Dr. Ramoray," Gabriel called into his earpiece, "do you still have access to the doors?"

"You're talking to Dr. Ramoray?" Cora asked as they ran.

"She sent Ricou," Gabriel said. "Turns out she's as unhappy with the event plan as we are."

They had entered a copse of trees and kept following the path. Gabriel saw Peter working the silver remote in his hand as he went. "*Kekada*'s coming online."

"We need to rendezvous as soon as we can get clear," Gabriel shouted. He huffed as he leapt over a planter. He heard the sounds of guards coming through the trees behind them as Misty pulled ahead.

They came out of the trees and saw the double doors of the hangar before them.

"We see it," Gabriel said. "Open the doors?"

"Done," Dr. Ramoray said.

The great double doors began to slowly swing open and Gabriel and Misty ran for them, turning sideways and pushing through.

The hangar was empty except for the *Dinas* vehicles

and the *Kekada*, which was vibrating on its legs, its nose tilted down. Gabriel looked up to his right to see the stairs leading up to the control room. Peter stuck his head out.

"We're here, shut 'em," Gabriel called. "Um, please."

"Absolutely," Dr. Ramoray said.

The hangar doors slammed shut.

"Now you'll need to let me know when you've gotten to the ship so I can flood—" Dr. Ramoray was cut off.

"Dr. Ramoray?" They were running toward the *Kekada* and Gabriel winced. They'd lost Dr. Ramoray. Meaning they'd lost her remote control of the hangar. Meaning even when they got to the ship, they wouldn't be able to flood the hangar so they could take the elevator out.

"This is the director," Minerva said in their ears. They reached the legs of the crab and Peter unlocked the iris. As it slid open Minerva went on. "Don't you think it would be better if you stayed?"

"Maybe for you," Gabriel said as he hauled himself up into the dive room. They got into the bridge and Cora headed toward the science station as he slammed into his chair. "Cameras," he said.

Peter was at his station and flicked the viewscreen on. In the control room, an operator stood staring through the window at them.

"Engines on?" Gabriel asked.

"Yes. What are we doing, Gabe?" Peter responded.

Gabriel thought. They didn't have a lot of options

inside a submarine. They had weapons that were supposed to shoot through water, not air, and the hangar was dry.

Just take it one thing at a time, he told himself. First, make sure no one could get to them.

"Misty," Gabriel called. "Fry the doors. Two torpedoes right against the door seam." When she stared back as if this were completely insane, he added, "Otherwise they'll catch up to us any second."

Misty took a moment to aim and said, "Away." Gabriel watched two of the missiles fly out from the *Kekada*. In the air they dropped slightly, finally sizzling across the floor. They hit the double doors perfectly and arcs of energy splayed like a spiderweb all across them.

Now they were alone.

Now what?

Alone except for the control room. Gabriel saw two more figures step in behind the glass. It was Minerva and Nils.

The ship rattled as it shook on the tiles of the hangar. He saw guards come in behind Minerva. Heading for the door out of the control room onto the stairs into the hangar.

Stop them. He needed time to think. "Don't," Gabriel said. "Don't come in."

They didn't stop. One of them had his hand on the door.

"Touch that door and we'll put a torpedo through the window you're standing behind," Gabriel said. He wouldn't. He didn't think so. But he needed to think.

They stopped.

"Options?" Gabriel asked the crew.

"Threaten them again," Peter said. "Tell them to flood the hangar and start the elevator."

"Will they?" Misty asked. "I don't think so."

"They won't," Cora agreed. She was watching Nils. Gabriel wondered how impossible this must be for her.

"I promise you I wouldn't actually shoot them," Gabriel said. He wanted her to know.

She looked back, her eyes sad. "Okay."

A dry hangar. And a dry red submarine.

Then Gabriel saw it. All in a flash. "Peter. How far can we go if we roll back on the back legs?"

Peter shook his head. "About a forty-five degree angle. We'll look like a begging dog."

"What are you thinking?" Misty asked.

"We have to shoot our way out," Gabriel said. "Shoot the elevator panel in the ceiling. It'll flood the hangar."

"But in the air, we can't shoot anything except straight. Straight up to hit the panels. And we can't get any steeper than forty-five degrees."

"We do it flipping over," Gabriel said. "Use the..."

Peter snapped his fingers and held out both hands. "Front legs, push down hard, strong, to propel us back. When they're off the ground, tilt back and put all power in the back legs, sending us straight up. For a second. *Less*—we'll be in the air for a blink. Then we'll fall over on our back," Peter said. "But by then you'll have shot the panel, so it won't be for long."

205

"Wait, we're doing what?" Cora asked, and her safety belt slammed around her as it did the rest of them.

"Watch pilots," the director said on the intercom so they could hear her. "Bring Dr. Ramoray here."

"What?" they heard Nils ask.

"Bring her here," Minerva said. "I want them to see her."

"This is about to get worse," Misty said.

"What are they going to do?" Cora asked.

Two pilots disappeared from the control room. That left one pilot, plus Nils, plus Minerva.

"Go," Gabriel said.

Peter worked the controls in front of them as the machinery in the legs whined. The ship rocked forward, the face nearly touching the floor. Then Gabriel's stomach lurched as the front legs coiled and snapped back, straightening out. The crab swung upward, and the rear legs bent until their knees touched the floor of the hangar.

"Misty, fire at will. Maximum charge."

They lunged, the legs forcing the crab ship upward. They lifted off. Just for a moment. The cameras showed the ceiling as the crab lurched heavily toward it, the engines howling in dry protest.

"Away," Misty said. Two torpedoes shot like bottle rockets out of the hull of the *Kekada*. They saw the torpedoes burst against the wide panel far above them. And then the crab ship began to fall, crunching down with a sickening lurch. They fell over backward.

Gabriel hung in his straps as the crab ship rocked on its back.

"Well," Peter said. "We're upside down again."

Cora asked, "Do you think…"

They heard a fierce crack. And then the weight of the ocean ripped the panel aside and thousands of tons of water rushed in.

On the viewscreen, which was upside down, they saw water filling the hangar. "Let's go," Gabriel said.

"Don't have to ask me twice," Peter said. They were upside down on the surface of the rising water and Peter swooped the ship backward and down, so close to the flooded floor that they nearly rammed into it. They all breathed easier, then, because they were right-side up once more as the water filled the room ever faster. "Just a few more seconds," Peter said. "Then we can say goodbye to the rats of MIM."

Peter took the *Kekada* over by the control room window. Minerva was staring at them, and for the first time, she seemed enraged.

"That should do it," Gabriel said. He meant that the hangar should be flooded by now. But he was also thinking that he had made another enemy.

Peter reared the ship back and they zipped up through the hangar and out the ruined door.

"Once you're above the canyons, engage the SC drive. Due north, give us distance." Gabriel tapped a button. "Nerissa?"

"We're on the way," his sister said.

"Not here. Meet us in the Bristol Channel. We'll send you coordinates to rendezvous."

"Copy. What's next?"

Gabriel shook his head. "We have to convince the UK that it's going to be invaded by giant snakes."

22

TWO HUNDRED MILES off the coast of Newfoundland, freezing waves chopped at Gabriel's feet as he walked with his crew across the walkway that extended between the *Kekada* and the *Nebula*. It was still the middle of the night, and the moon was high behind the clouds. The wind bit at his face and made his limbs sting with cold.

Nerissa waited grimly on the other end of the walkway, her peacoat pulled around her and flapping in the wind. One by one, Nerissa extended a hand and helped each of them up onto the hull and to the entry hatch. She paused at Cora and looked at Gabriel. "You decided..."

Cora took her hand. "I'm here because...I need to be here. And because if I can keep anyone from being hurt—including the City...I need to."

They gathered in Nerissa's sanctum sanctorum near the *Nebula*'s bridge. There was room for everyone around the wooden table, and Nerissa stood at the head. "Okay," she said. "What are we looking at?"

Misty brought out her phone and flicked it. The image of the battle plan appeared on a screen. The targets. "One against Penarth Pier. Two against the dam. Three inside the bay attacking Mermaid Quay."

"What are those images supposed to be?" She pointed to the gray shapes. "You said something about snakes?"

"They are," Cora said. "Genetically engineered sea serpents who can eat and digest metal and plastic, anything man-made. And they can be controlled by us. I'm guessing Minerva will direct them herself."

Gabriel was thinking of the blinky boxes on their necks. "How will she control them?"

"They'll use a ship," Cora said. "They won't be able to control the serpents all the way from the City on the bottom. Once Kaa got away, his controls fell apart pretty quickly. So probably Minerva will be aboard a command ship sending signals, impulses to the serpents. The *O'Connell* is the only one that will work."

"And for protection?" Nerissa asked.

"A team of fighters, small craft," Gabriel said. "Commanded by the Watch, their pilots."

"You have to *promise* me you won't destroy them," Cora said. "Nils is wrong to follow Minerva's plan, but he's got a good heart. And I owe him everything." Gabriel understood. Nils had taken her under his wing.

"Our concern is stopping this attack," Nerissa said. "It has to be."

"I'm just saying..."

"We'll do our best," Gabriel said.

"It's not our concern." Nerissa used the word again, sternly this time. "Your...brother, for want of a better word, is heading into battle. And if he were out there on the ocean attacking ships, maybe I wouldn't even care. But *that*?" She pointed at the snakes in the bay. "We can't let that happen. It would rain fire on all of us, especially the Nemos. So no, I can't guarantee his safety." She looked at all of them. "When is this to happen?"

"Today, ten A.M.," Peter said. "Just hours from now. Thanksgiving morning."

"If this were America that might help because everyone would be indoors," Misty said. "But this is the UK, so it doesn't."

They couldn't handle this on their own, Gabriel thought. "We should call the authorities. What's the...What's the British equivalent of whatever they have in the US, Naval Intelligence?"

"You always think in navy," Misty said. She seemed to be accessing everything she knew about the world of spies, which Gabriel suspected was where she ultimately hoped to be. "In the US, it would be the Department of Homeland

Security. And in the United Kingdom, it would be MI5. Security services."

"MI5. Okay." Nerissa looked like she'd swallowed something bad. Like she was handling something that might poison her. She rubbed her face. "So, let's say we call MI5—who, if I need to remind you, regard *us* as dangerous—and tell them, uh, in the morning tomorrow, a bunch of snakes are going to attack Cardiff Bay. But just so you know, the snakes will call it Tiger Bay."

"The snakes don't talk." Cora rolled her eyes.

"What a relief!" Peter said. He scoffed, taking off his glasses and gesturing with them. "But I've seen those things, they can easily take out the pier. And they can crawl. Up onto land. Guys, our families are in Cardiff *right now*. We have to warn *them*. We have to warn *everybody*."

"Maybe," Nerissa said. "If the governments weren't likely to blame it on us, we'd rescue your families because you're allies of the Nemos and leave this place and not come back."

"Nerissa!" Gabriel was shocked. "You'd just..."

"Just what, Gabriel? We're defenders of the ocean. We're not citizens of the United Kingdom *or* the United States. Half the navies of the world want to blow our ships out of the water. We don't owe them anything. And frankly, Cora's city has a point. The governments of the world have not really served us."

"Thousands of people could die," Misty said.

"And that is the only reason I'm even having this conversation," Nerissa said. "That and I'm not crazy about a world where a Victorian cruise ship will try to have a say in where *I* go."

"Well, I'm glad *your* priorities are in order," Peter said.

"I hear you," Nerissa said, shrugging. Not like she thought it was a good idea. "You want to warn the UK, let's do it. It'll give them some time to prepare a defense."

Nerissa led Gabriel to her desk. It was a huge piece of dark, almost black wood with a stylized *N* carved into the front. On the desk was a globe that looked antique, but had a tiny shining dot indicating the *Nebula*'s position.

Nerissa pushed aside the black ergonomic chair behind the desk and turned toward the silver screen behind it. She and Gabriel leaned back against the desk. Nerissa put her hands in her pockets and cleared her throat. "*Nebula*, ship to land call."

An automated male voice responded, "Who do you want to call?"

"UK…Ministry of defense…Security services…Terrorist threat…hotline."

Gabriel was impressed. "You've done this before?"

She shrugged. "Nope. They're keywords."

The automated voice said, "It's ringing."

They heard a trilling of bells and a *clack* as they connected. A chipper, female, British voice answered, "You've reached the hotline. What do you wish to report?"

Gabriel thought Nerissa was going to talk, but she looked at him. He cleared his throat. No problem. He'd once negotiated with a naval captain not to blow up the Lodgers. "Ma'am, this is Cap..." He paused. Was he really going to call himself Captain Nemo? "Ma'am, I'm calling about a terrorist threat that we learned of."

"I see," she said. Not mocking. Not doubting. Neutral. "Can you tell me about the threat?"

"Yes. I found plans by an organization that shows they intend to attack Cardiff Bay and Penarth Pier tomorrow at ten."

A pause. "Are you in a safe location?"

"Yes. I'm not there anymore." He looked back at the crew, who were watching him. Misty's phone had the picture she'd taken.

Gabriel heard brisk snapping, like the woman was summoning someone from nearby. "Go on, what kind of attack?"

"It's... animal."

"Animal?"

Gabriel winced. Nerissa leaned toward him. "By all means," she whispered. "Do go on."

Gabriel inhaled. Said it all in a breath. "Six giant genetically engineered sea serpents will be deployed to take out the pier, the dam, and Mermaid Quay."

The woman sounded like she was writing. "Six... giant... genetically engineered... sea serpents." She cleared her throat. "And how giant?"

Gabriel thought, *How giant?* "Ah, sixty feet. Give or take."

"Excellent. Well, we shall certainly make good use of this information. Goodbye!" Brisk and cheerful.

"No, ma'am, this is serious."

"No, young man," she said with a stern tone. "This is a serious line for serious people. Now, you've had your laugh, but we must work."

Click.

Gabriel was shocked. No one ever didn't take him seriously, what was she thinking? "Get them back," he said.

"Don't bother." Nerissa chuckled. "That lady was pretty cool, I'm surprised she kept you on as long as she did." Nerissa turned back to face the group. "Guys? Do you know what this desk is?"

Everyone looked at one another. No answers.

"This desk came from a Nemoship that was used to rescue President Franklin Roosevelt in a secret mission during World War II. We weren't citizens then, either, but we knew which side to choose. We weren't about to let Nazis rule the seas. We do choose sides when we have to." She studied the globe for a second and then looked back at the crew. "And that's what we have to do now. We're going to have to defend Cardiff and put a stop to *Dinas Nautilus*'s plan."

"What about our families?" Peter asked. He looked pretty ill himself.

"We warn them to stay inside," Nerissa said. "And there are no other Nemoships in this area, no one that can get here by tomorrow morning. So it's the *Nebula* and the *Kekada*. Where is *Dinas* now?"

"Why?" Cora asked.

Nerissa spoke quietly. "For the greater good, we have to consider going back and telling them to call off their plans, or we have no choice but to attack them."

"They'll have moved," Cora said. "The moment we ran. You saw what they did when they were spotted by the Maelstrom. *Dinas* survives by moving constantly, and when they're discovered, moving right away."

"And we damaged their hangar," Gabriel said. "So that should cause them some headaches."

Nerissa spun the globe and aimed the British Isles at the group, coming around the desk to put her thumb on the water way below and east of Ireland. "So they'll be somewhere below Bristol Channel, and send their attack into Cardiff."

"We have more than the *Nebula* and *Kekada*. Is there a runabout on the *Nebula*, something with torpedoes?" Gabriel asked.

"Yes," Nerissa said. "*Aronnax II*. It can carry four torpedoes."

Gabriel went to one of the screens and tapped its side, and it turned white. He drew and wrote with his finger as he thought. He drew a diagonal line running from northeast to southwest. "This is the shore. At the top is the dam ... and behind it, Cardiff Bay, which is a lake full of people, with Mermaid Quay on the other side of that. South down the shore is the pier."

He wrote *pier*. "One snake here so it needs a ship. This is the smallest threat, so ..."

"But there will people all over that, too," Cora said. It was her favorite spot.

"We have three ships. One, *Aronnax*, will protect the pier." Next to *pier* he wrote *A*. "That will be me and Cora."

"You're leaving the *Kekada*?" Misty asked.

"We have to." He wrote *dam* and a *K*. "*You'll* command *Kekada*. Peter can work the legs like nobody's business. Two snakes are gonna stop and chew up the locks. They do that, it'll destroy the lake and wreak havoc inside, and possibly flood Cardiff. So we need you up and crawling around on the dam to defend it."

"That sounds cool," Peter said.

Gabriel looked back at his sister, who was studying the diagram intently. "That leaves the three that will be headed straight toward the dam, clearly intended to go right over it and into the lake. They can't even reach the dam. The *Nebula* will focus on them." Gabriel added an *N*.

"So you're leaving the biggest fight to the *Nebula*?" Nerissa asked. "Makes sense."

"Yours is the main attack." Gabriel nodded as he stepped back. "But it's not the biggest fight. They've divided this up to make it hard, to prove a point." He turned around. "Well?"

"There's something else," Cora said. "We can't destroy the snakes."

Peter scoffed. "Excuse me?"

"They're just giant creatures. They wouldn't do any of this if they weren't being forced. We need to destroy the control boxes on their necks. But try not to hurt them."

"I..." Nerissa shook her head.

"They're *innocent*."

"I don't know if we can guarantee that," Gabriel said. The second time the phrase had been used.

"I...agree with Cora," Nerissa said. "We protect sea creatures. Genetically engineered or not, they're not at fault."

Gabriel nodded. "All right. So that's the plan."

"Good." Misty stepped forward to the diagram. "Where'd you learn this stuff?"

"Nemolab," Gabriel and his sister muttered.

"I gotta spend a summer there." She turned around and said to Gabriel, "So this *Aronnax*? I guess you have a couple of hours to learn how it runs."

"And we need rest," Gabriel said. He yawned the moment he thought of it. They had been running for two nights. They all had to be exhausted. "Two hours to replenish anything the ships need and for me to learn how the *Aronnax* runs. And then two hours rest." He looked at Cora, who still wore her leather jacket and Elizabethan flotation collar. "And we gotta get you a Nemo jacket."

23

A FEW HOURS later, Gabriel and Cora were side by side in the silver *Aronnax* as it zipped through the water toward the pier. The *Aronnax* was nearly as long as the *Kekada*, and looked like a small version of the *Nebula*, swooped at the front and back with a wide nose that made it look vaguely like a hammerhead shark. Instead of using cameras, they looked out through Nemoglass cockpit windows as the pier filtered into view through the murky water.

The intercom opened up with Nerissa's voice. "We've got them on the scopes."

Along the bottom of the windows was a screen that ran their length, and Cora put the sonar up next to a drone view of the pier, which teamed with midmorning foot traffic.

On the sonar screen they could see three long shapes.

One headed their way, two toward the dam. Cora shook her head. "Where are the other three?"

"Don't know yet," Nerissa said.

"We're headed for the dam," Misty called.

On the sonar, Gabriel could see the *Kekada* moving in the bay, not far off from the dam. On the screen, the clouds had separated, and it was a sunny morning. The ocean was blue and choppy. There were people on the beach that ran along the cliffs by the pier. People walking along the dam. Sailboats on the lake.

"Swing us around," Gabriel said, and Cora swung the joystick controller of the *Aronnax*, putting their aft section to the pier. They hung there at fifty feet below the surface. Watching the shape undulate across the sonar screen.

"Go to meet it," he said. He had the weapons menu up on a tablet mounted and angled before him. As the *Aronnax* began to move toward the approaching shape, he chose the portside torpedo tube and set the power low, but not too low. "Thirty percent," he said aloud. "Aim for the heat signature of the control boxes. Thirty percent should damage the boxes but not the snake." He was thinking of how hard the box on Kaa had been to hit with the rifles and hoped that he was figuring it right.

"Copy," Misty said. She was running weapons on the *Kekada* so that Peter could pay attention to piloting. "Nothing's coming up yet."

On Gabriel's own screen, there was still nothing to

target. Cora had helped them, even lending them the *Dinas Nautilus* belt she wore, which opened doors and so forth, so they could use it to take a guess at what the signature would look like. The weapons were ready. The snake just had to get close enough.

On the sonar, he saw the two snakes still two miles away from the *Kekada* and the dam. If Misty could hit them in the water, Peter wouldn't have to do any crazy crawling around on the dam after all.

Two miles to his own. Closer.

"Time to our position, ninety seconds," Cora said.

"Ready." Everyone echoed their readiness.

In the distance, in the water, Gabriel saw a shape. He magnified the window. A shadow. Swishing.

The snake turned to its right, the bead on the sonar screen suddenly pinging off at a north angle.

"What, what's it doing?" Cora shouted. It was swimming northward and away, doing sixty knots.

"Follow it!" Gabriel shouted. Cora slammed the accelerator forward and they started to move.

"Where'd they go?" Misty called. "Our snakes just disappeared."

"You've got ours headed right at you," Gabriel said as he watched the snake that was supposed to come to him head toward the *Kekada* and the dam. The two that had been headed toward there had already dropped off the scope completely.

And then the snake he was pursuing disappeared.

Nerissa swore in his ear from the *Nebula*. "They changed their plan."

Of course. Because wouldn't he? If someone had come across it and maybe taken a picture of it? *Mobilis in Mobili.* Change in the changes. Minerva was following the code. But where were they?

"They must have gone deep," Peter said. "To the bottom, just to stay off sonar."

"We're headed to join you," Gabriel said. "Ours gave up on the pier. Go deep, look for them." As he said this, Cora put the *Aronnax* into a dive and they dropped to two hundred feet, moving fast. Still nothing. "Where are they?"

He could see the *Kekada* up ahead and Cora swung them alongside as they pushed out toward the sea.

Nothing.

And then a huge dot appeared on the sonar screen, a dot with a large tail. Coming up from below. Just to the north of them. Gabriel took it in and called out, "The snakes are massed together! They're coming."

"What's the plan?" Peter said as the *Kekada* swooped ahead of the *Aronnax*.

"We've got ships," Nerissa called. Up from below now, Gabriel saw a large dot out in the bay, moving toward the shore, with the *Nebula* in their way. Six smaller ships zipped before it, protecting the command ship. "The *O'Connell* and the pilots of the Watch are here."

Now Gabriel saw the snakes. Coming swiftly into view, they were close on one another, one in the center and five around it, moving in perfect coordination. He saw the open mouths.

"Same plan," Gabriel called. "I'll take two on the starboard side, Misty, aim for two on the port."

The box signature lit up on his targeting screen and he swept the target with his finger until it pointed to one of the snakes on the right of the mass. They were coming fast now.

He fired. The missile whipped out, joined after a moment by one from Misty. They danced through the water, headed for the snakes. One of the six mouths dropped, snapping at Gabriel's missile as it came toward it. The missile burst and energy danced over its head. The mass kept moving, the snake staying in formation.

Misty had better luck. Her missile hit the box of one on the left and the box exploded, the snake spinning away, snapping in all directions. It dipped down and up at the *Kekada*, snapping its great jaws. "Whoa," Gabriel heard Peter cry as he spun the *Kekada* out of the way.

And the snakes were past.

"After them," Gabriel said. Cora jerked the *Aronnax* downward as the snake whose control box Misty had blown swept over them, its eyes flicking as it fled. "Nerissa, everybody: They're *all* going for the dam." Probably Minerva's plan would still be: Damage the dam and wreak havoc on the lake. Probably.

They were in pursuit now, five snakes still moving like an undulating torpedo.

Still not separated. The submarines had to get closer to do the job. From behind, there were five tails whipping wildly and they couldn't possibly hope to hit the small targets on the snakes themselves.

"I suggest a new plan, Gabriel," Nerissa said. "We need to blow the command ship out of the water."

"No!" Cora shouted.

"We don't have any choice," Nerissa said. At this point Gabriel had to agree with her. On the sonar screen, the snakes were closing on the dam.

"It won't work," Cora said. "Minerva will be controlling the snakes, but if you blow up her ship, they'll just keep going.

"You'd have to take the controller. You can't just blow it up."

The *Aronnax* was still moving toward the dam, which rose ahead of them as a mile-long wall in the water. The silvery snakes hit the wall and begin to climb.

What now? What now? They couldn't target the boxes. They were on the other side of the snakes. And Gabriel had promised not to hurt them. He cursed *Dinas Nautilus* for doing something so cruel as creating these creatures and then using them for evil.

"Peter and Misty?" he called.

"Protect the dam?" Peter asked. On the aerial view, he saw five giant snakes come out of the water, just a few yards from the top of the dam. The water was right at the top.

Already the *Kekada* was swooping up as it neared the wall, the legs coming up from beneath it as it pushed up toward the surface. Gabriel saw the black face of the crab pop up, its legs grabbing on to the top of the dam about forty yards from the snakes.

He saw people on the walkway at the top of the dam, running.

"Yes—Cora, bring us about. Nerissa?"

"Yep."

"We're going after the command ship. We have to board it."

Cora nodded and they swung again, headed back toward the *O'Connell*. Here and there in the bay were regular ships, fishing boats, cargo ships. All unawares. And zipping underwater were the pilot ships. "I wonder which of those is Nils," she said.

"Stay low," Gabriel said as they got closer to the *O'Connell* on the scopes.

"One minute away."

One of the pilot ships on the far right was close enough to fire. Cora called out, "Torpedo in the water."

"Evasive," Gabriel said, and they zipped down. The torpedo twisted toward them and missed them by a yard. "Top speed. We can't ram the *O'Connell*, so we need to get behind it." Cora pushed them forward. The milk-white ship came into view and they soared down past it. Cora brought the *Aronnax* about fifty feet farther down and started to come up.

As they did so, Gabriel slapped the panel in front of him. "Options?"

"What?"

"Options. It's what we do," he told Cora. "Misty, are you listening? How do we board that ship?"

Misty's voice sounded forced. "We're a...little busy." On the screen, the *Kekada* was up on the dam, using its legs to swat at snakes. It sent one of them flying into the sea. But Gabriel could see that two had already made it over the dam into the lake. Headed for Mermaid Quay.

"We can't shoot it open," Cora said. "They're a hundred feet down. It would rupture and maybe explode."

"Is there a top hatch?"

"Yes," she said. "But I don't see how you get into it. Not underwater."

Gabriel cursed. One of the pilot ships was nearing them and swooped over their nose as they leveled off in pursuit of the *O'Connell*. They loosed a torpedo and Cora cried out.

"Countermeasures," Gabriel said, and looked. On his menu system he saw COUNTERMEASURES—1 and fired them out. The little canisters zipped away from the nose of the *Aronnax*. The torpedo found them and exploded, the shock wave rocking the *Aronnax*.

Now the weapons systems said COUNTERMEASURES—0. An emergency tool, one time only. This ship wasn't meant to see battle except maybe to escape from one.

But they were nearly as long as the *O'Connell*.

Suddenly Gabriel saw it. How to get in. But it would take steps.

"Nerissa, I need *Nebula* to focus on the pilots," he said.

"You have a plan?"

"Yes. Just keep them off us."

"Copy," Nerissa said. He trusted her. He could turn to the next thing. He turned to Cora. "Put this ship right under the *O'Connell*. It'll make it harder for the pilot ships to fire on us."

Cora nodded, aiming the *Aronnax* at the tail of the *O'Connell*. "That makes sense."

"And then bash them from below and push them to the surface."

"Whoa, whoa," Peter said from the *Kekada*. "Get . . . off," he cried as he swatted one of the snakes onscreen. "Gabriel, we talked about this with the lifeboats. You could crack the *Aronnax*."

"I don't *think* so," Gabriel said. "Because *O'Connell* is a submarine with its own buoyancy."

"You think, this is based on what you *think*?" Cora asked, swiveling toward him.

He was rummaging underneath the panel. "That's how everything interesting happens . . . Nerissa, how's the top hull integrity on this thing?" Finally he found a lever and pulled open a long hatch. Inside he saw a pair of rebreathers.

Nerissa came back, "Not as bad as the *Kekada*."

"Do it," Gabriel said. Cora was coming down as one of the pilots zipped alongside. This time it was Nils.

Maybe it was because it was Cora with Gabriel. Gabriel couldn't divine the Watch leader's thoughts. But in that moment, Nils didn't fire on them. He could have, and that was his last chance.

Because now they were coming up underneath the *O'Connell*. Cora put the *Aronnax* right underneath, where the pilots couldn't shoot without risking their own ship.

"Wait," Cora said, "even if we push them up, we're still down here."

Gabriel put one rebreather around his neck and handed the other to Cora. "Nope, we'll be in the water," he said. "You've got to come with me. But not yet." He pointed up. "Push them up."

Cora pulled back the stick and the *Aronnax* groaned as the hull slammed into the *O'Connell*. They kept moving along the bay, but she called out the elevation. "One hundred...ninety-five..."

"When we're at thirty, they'll be on the surface," Gabriel said. "Let me know when we reach fifty, because that's when we've got to flood the *Aronnax* so we can swim out. Anything below that will be too dangerous for us." He pulled a pair of goggles from a hatch above his head and put them on. "Here's what we're going to do. The water will be too choppy right against the sub for us to just climb up, so we need to ride away from the ships and come back on the surface to board the *O'Connell*. So we gotta put together the stuff we need for that."

"Gabriel," Peter called, "the snakes are in the bay." On the aerial screen, the *Kekada* leapt off the dam and into the lake. "We're in pursuit."

"Sixty-five feet," Cora called. The white ship above them was so close to the surface that they could see sunlight.

Gabriel looked back at the inner hull and the *Aronnax*'s various equipment. A latticework of straps lined the hull, on which lots of gear was fastened. Harpoon guns. Pincer rifles. And a Katana.

Gabriel unfastened from his seat and ran back toward a harpoon gun, long, with a four-pronged harpoon on the end. Deadly and solid. He called to Cora, "You think this'll grab on to the hide of the *O'Connell*?"

She nodded. "I think so." Then, looking down, "We're at fifty feet."

Gabriel returned to the controls as Cora unfastened from her seat. He talked fast. "The *O'Connell* is at the surface," he said. The engines groaned against the weight of the ship above them. Gabriel brought up a diagram of the *Aronnax* that showed its hull strength in real time. The blue outline of the hull sang out with warnings. The top was being pressed and misshapen. It would hold for now. The *O'Connell* had to be suffering much the same way as they pressed up against it. It was slightly rounded, so it didn't lay perfectly flat against the top of the *Aronnax*, and its hull would be warping. But he had them captured. They were as stuck as if he had laid them on the ground. "I'm setting *Aronnax* to maintain this depth and speed by continuing to press upward against their weight."

He found the menu for the rear hatch. The hatch was wide, big enough to roll a Nemorover into. "You ready for the next step?"

She nodded and they ran for the back with its plethora of equipment and straps.

Gabriel grabbed a pair of pincer rifles, one for him and one for Cora. He handed her one. "Remember," he said. They strapped the guns around them. "They're non-lethal." They had been over the rifles, just in case, during her two-hour tutorial aboard the *Nebula*. "But the *O'Connell* might not know that."

For just a moment he wished that he had Misty with him. He was used to having her there when he had to run around with pincer rifles. But Misty had her own job to do, and this was his.

He turned his attention back to the harpoon gun. It was held with thick Velcro to the straps on the wall. He unfastened it and handed it to Cora. "Hold this against the body of the Katana. We need to fasten it to the side."

While Cora held the gun in place, Gabriel rolled the Velcro straps around the body of the little vehicle, clasping the harpoon in place, one at the front of the gun, one in the back. Tugged on it. It would hold.

Then he unfastened the Katana and it rocked in place on the floor. "Hop on," Gabriel said. Cora got on the back of the Katana, holding it with her legs while she stayed upright by holding the straps on the wall.

"You ready?" Gabriel asked.

She pulled her goggles down over her eyes. "Aye." They put on their rebreathers and gave each other the thumbs-up.

Gabriel hustled back to the front. He grabbed a handle on the ceiling and hit the button for the hatch. The wide door began to open, hinges moving, water spraying against the hull. The water began to flow and rise fast in the *Aronnax*.

The water reached over their heads and Gabriel swam back to Cora once again, sliding onto the Katana by the open hatch.

He kicked the side of the little craft and it thrummed to life. Time to go. They swept out through the open door into the sea.

Gabriel drove the Katana directly out of the wake of the engines and up, to burst through the surface like a dolphin. They landed on choppy waves and inertia took him about twenty yards farther than he wanted. Frustrated, he yanked the Katana around.

The *O'Connell* was half surfaced, spray coming off its whale-skin-like hull. Gabriel throttled the Katana and danced across the choppy water, aiming straight for the *O'Connell*'s side.

The spray next to the ship was heavy. Gabriel got within twenty feet, the Katana fighting and bucking with them, and he reached down and triggered the harpoon gun.

The four-pronged harpoon shot through the water, trailing a silver cord that whipped and shone in the spray as it went. The harpoon stuck deep in the hull.

"Hang on," Gabriel said.

The cord went taut and the Katana yanked forward, wrenching Gabriel and Cora as the Katana's engines fought to keep the vehicle upright. The forward motion of the *O'Connell* dragged them back instantly, right toward the hull. Exactly as Gabriel wanted.

The body of the *O'Connell* was about thirty feet wide, smoothly sloped. Gabriel whipped the Katana left away from the ship, and then right, pulling up. The Katana bucked in the spray and they were up, sliding onto the top of the hull.

"Roll," Gabriel said. And he tilted the Katana and they rolled off onto the top. It was flat enough that they had a good six feet to lay on for a moment. The Katana pulled away and back to the side and clattered by itself into the churning water as the ship carried it along.

Cora got to her knees, pointing at a hump toward the nose of the craft. "There's the hatch."

They scuttled low, on elbows and toes, along the hull, which felt to Gabriel like crawling on rubber.

Finally they reached the mound and Cora indicated a shining panel next to the door. She grabbed her belt and tore it off, holding the buckle up to the sensor.

For a moment Gabriel wondered if *Dinas Nautilus* had already turned off Cora's general access codes. Nerissa would have. But the panel split open and, in two perfect halves, disappeared into the hull.

Gabriel and Cora looked down into the *O'Connell*. Then Gabriel said, "Let's go."

An arc of energy zapped past Gabriel's shoulder, narrowly missing Cora and glancing off the hull and into the water. Gabriel and Cora looked back.

Nils lay at the tail of the *O'Connell*, water streaming off his body. His ship moved nearby off the portside, where Nils's copilot still ran the ship.

"That's far enough," Nils said.

"Gabriel, you have to hurry," Peter said from the *Kekada*. "Those things are moving across the water. We're chasing after them."

"We don't have time for this," Gabriel shouted as he turned over. He tried to maintain a grip on the hull with his heels and one hand while he raised his own rifle. "We're stopping this ship."

Nils waved the rifle at Cora and Gabriel, one at a time. "Get away from that hatch and into the water."

"Nils, please," Cora shouted. She crawled a step toward Nils, reaching out one hand. She was in the way—Gabriel couldn't have shot Nils if he tried unless he was willing to hit Cora. "Please. This isn't who we are!" she shouted.

"Do you think that's up to you?" Nils eyes blazed under his drenched hair. "Do you think I believe in everything she does? But she's helped us survive."

"We're done talking," Gabriel said. "We're going down into this ship."

"Gabriel, hurry!" Misty called.

Cora answered, "He's on his way." Then she rose, running for Nils. Gabriel watched her fling herself bodily at Nils, putting her arms around him and battering him back. They tumbled off the tail of the *O'Connell* and into the wake.

For a split second Gabriel thought about diving after them and helping Cora fight off Nils, but he knew better. She had given Gabriel time and space to do his job. He needed to use it.

He began climbing down the hatch, whispering, "Cora knocked Nils into the water and went with him. As soon as someone can, go after her."

He moved fast, dropping into a corridor of wood and brass. He passed a little plaque on the wall that said DANIEL O'CONNELL—MIM.

"Why are we on the surface?" Minerva was calling. Gabriel reached an anteroom behind the bridge. Through a porthole in a door he could see Minerva with two pilots. She was wearing large goggles like Cora's and had a long, smooth, silver controller in her hand. She swung the controller wildly, gesturing outside.

The helmsman wrung his hands. "They're *under* us, ma'am."

They hadn't seen him through the porthole yet. Gabriel felt his nerves jagging wildly, and he had to grip the rifle to try not to shake. He was going to have to do this by himself. One thing at a time. *Get in, get control of the snakes.*

"Everyone's hands off the controls," Gabriel shouted as he pushed in.

The helmsman and ops officer gasped and put up their hands when they saw the pincer rifle.

The screen behind the crew was oval-shaped and intricately adorned with a gold band, rather like a golden ivy. It was very Nemo.

The top left quarter of the screen showed the sonar and all the ships around. Three of the pilot ships were circling around the *Nebula* while Nils's ship was still near the *O'Connell*. The final two Watch ships were closer to the shore, probably looking for a chance to engage the *Kekada*.

The top right showed what was directly outside: water splashing against the *O'Connell*'s front cameras as it sat surfaced atop the *Aronnax*. The lower left quarter showed an aerial view of Cardiff Bay, where the five remaining serpents were moving through the water, their heads up like a bunch of Loch Ness Monsters. The lower right quarter showed thousands of people gathered on the promenade in *Dinas Nautilus*. The bottom of the image said LIVE. They were watching.

Minerva looked back. "Ignore him. Ops, see if you can't reprogram a torpedo to go deep and come up to blow up the ship below us. Helmsman? Take this boy into custody."

"That's not how this is going to go," Gabriel said. "All three of you, against the wall. Minerva, drop the controller."

"Get serious," Minerva said. "I'll do no such thing."

In Gabriel's ear Misty spoke, "Gabriel, the snakes are very close to the other side," she said. "There are people *everywhere* on the beach." On the screen, he could see them. Swimmers were beginning to flee the water. They were scurrying like ants as the snakes churned their way up. He needed to turn them around.

"Drop it, now," Gabriel shouted.

"Who do you think you are?"

He pulled the trigger. The rifle jolted in his hand as an arc of energy sizzled past Minerva, arcing over her shoulder and sizzling her hair. She raised her hand, dropping the controller. He wasted no time lunging for it.

But the moment he lowered the rifle the helmsman was on him, grabbing Gabriel by the shoulders and slamming him into the deck. The controller punched up painfully against Gabriel's chest as he landed on it and rolled, kicking the helmsman out of the way. He grabbed the rifle and fired. He was done. *This thing is built to stun. Let's hope that's true.*

Gabriel swept the bridge with arcs of pincer energy, catching the three of them across the chest. Each of them shook and dropped, but as Minerva fell, she went down on her knees and clawed toward Gabriel, her nails extended.

"You...," she spat as her eyes fluttered, "are a *disgrace*." And then her eyes rolled back as she fell to the floor.

"Well, you're no Nemo." He scrambled out of the way as she landed in a heap. He didn't have time to check and see if she or the other two were alive, though he really hoped they were. He got to his knees and rose, moving to the screen with the controller.

Gabriel looked again at the aerial view. The snakes were coming up out of the water. He saw people running and tripping, tiny silhouettes in many colors.

"They're reaching the beach!" Misty called urgently.

Gabriel held up the controller but saw that it had nothing he could manipulate. It was ergonomic enough that he could tell what was the handle, but the silver blob at the end did nothing. He realized it probably had a menu he could only see through goggles.

He turned around and grabbed Minerva's goggles, pulling them on.

The menu that swam before him in the air was unreadable. He saw multiple screens upon screens of text and shifting three-dimensional Xs that reminded him of gyro-scopes. He was sure he could understand it eventually, probably in about a week.

On the beach, snakes were moving onto the sand. One of them appeared to be snapping at a giant umbrella and shaking it in its mouth as people ran. The *Kekada* was wad-ing up out of the water on its mechanical legs, battering at one of the snakes with one of the legs.

Distantly he heard Peter yell, "Cables!" and Gabriel saw one of the *Kekada*'s grappling lines shoot out to wrap around a telephone pole, just to try to put up some kind of barrier, anything to keep them from moving farther up the beach. He heard screaming.

"I don't know how to work this," he said aloud into his headset. "Cora, are you out there?"

No response.

Then, a cough.

"I'm alive," came her answer. "But I can't reach you." Of course, because they were probably half a mile away from her by now. "Nils fled."

Gabriel saw the other pilot ships, spreading out.

"Can you tell me how to use this thing?" On the screen, a snake was crawling over the *Kekada* as Peter and Misty fought, swatting one of the snakes aside while another gnawed on the hull. One was crawling toward a skating rink, trailing the ropes and silver posts of a queue for one of the vendors. One of them batted a cotton-candy cart out of the way with its nose, sending the cart flying as people ran in every direction.

"They can turn it off by remote," Cora said. He heard water lapping around her. "From the control room."

Gabriel looked at the screen showing the people of *Dinas Nautilus* watching. "I thought you said they can't control them from there."

"They can't. But they can sever the connection. Reset. But you'll never be able to control the snakes again."

"But if we do that, then what?" Gabriel shouted.

"Just try something!" Peter called. The *Kekada* was lunging across the beach, Peter throwing the ship between the snakes and several people.

"They're sea snakes," Cora said. "They don't want to be on a beach any more than you want them to."

That had to be it. Gabriel turned to the screen that said LIVE. The people were practically cowering. He understood. He had knocked out their director and taken over their ship.

"This is Gabriel Nemo calling *Dinas Nautilus*," he said. "The control room in particular. Because I know you're watching, too."

On the beach view, Gabriel saw Misty drop out of the *Kekada*. She had a pincer rifle in her hand, and she was tiny and screaming as she swept arcs of energy all around her, stumbling and running across the sand. She blasted a snake back before it bit a man who was running. She turned and fired and turned and fired.

"I need you to reset the connection to the serpents," he said. "This mission is over."

"No, Captain Nemo," came the voice of Nils. So he had made it back to his ship. On the screen, he was heading once more toward where Gabriel was on the *O'Connell*. "You're going to stand down."

"Nils, think of it," Gabriel said. He looked at the crowd. "All of you. You've lived in secrecy and you've tried to live according to the rules of Nemo. Of *Mobilis in Mobili*. Minerva led you in the wrong direction. It doesn't mean she was evil. But she got off track. I've lived my life trying to find the path that my ancestor Captain Nemo meant for us. And I do that knowing that he, too, got terribly off track. If you continue on this path, you will bring destruction on yourself. Killing the drylanders won't make them stop. You won't save the ocean. You'll only destroy yourselves. Reset. Reset and run."

At his feet, Minerva and the two crewmen were still out cold. There was no one who could help. Misty was staggering, firing, trying to keep the snakes on the beach.

And then Nils spoke again.

"Do it, control," Nils said. "On the order of the commander of the Watch. Pilots, stand down."

A pause, then a voice came back from the City. "Are you sure?"

"Affirmative," Nils answered. His ship was still coming

toward the *O'Connell*, the others arranged around his and following.

"Aye, aye, Commander," came the response.

On the screen, Misty fired her rifle as she backed against a pair of garbage barrels. She knocked them over and fell back, scrambling. She knelt against one of them as a snake above her reared up, opening its mouth as it prepared to lunge toward her.

Gabriel felt the controller jolt in his hand and saw the menus visible in the goggles suddenly collapse in on themselves with a fragile-sounding, staccato *zakt*.

The snake stopped.

They all stopped.

"What…," Misty called through the headset. She got up, staggering back, holding the rifle.

The snakes swayed, each of them in place. Peter echoed Misty as the *Kekada* backed away from the snake it was fighting.

And then one at a time the snakes began to move, shaking their heads and circling away. Gabriel watched the one near Misty turn, moving toward the water.

"The snakes are turning back," Misty said. "They're turning *back*!"

Gabriel called, "Nils?" He watched the shapes on the sonar headed their way. "Nils, are you there?"

The ship turned off to starboard, no longer on a collision course with the *O'Connell*.

The snakes had reached the sea now, slipping into the water.

"You've got another chance," Gabriel said. "I suggest you take *Dinas Nautilus* and disappear for a while. The authorities won't be hearing about you from us."

Finally Nils came back. "You still have our ship. And our director. If that's what she will still be."

"I should turn her over to the UK," Gabriel said. He sighed and turned the *O'Connell* in the direction of Cora, who floated a mile back. He saw her waving onscreen, tiny against the flickering daytime waves. "But my concern was the snakes. Nerissa?"

"The pilots of the Watch have broken off," Nerissa said. "You have a way off that thing?"

"I do." Gabriel slowed the *O'Connell* and let it drift. He spoke into the *O'Connell*'s radio one last time. "This is your command ship, Nils. Come and get it."

He left the unconscious crewmen and climbed out the hatch to find the Katana he'd harpooned to the side. The ship was still riding atop the flooded *Aronnax*.

Within three minutes he'd taken the Katana and ridden it out to meet Cora, and together they rode back to the *Aronnax*. They boarded the little sub through the same hatch they'd left and piloted it away still flooded as Nils's ship arrived.

As Gabriel used the pumps to blast the water out of the sub, Cora watched the sonar screen in silence. He watched her reach once toward the intercom to say something, and then she decided not to.

One by one Gabriel checked in with Peter and Misty and Nerissa, relieved to hear they were all okay.

As the *Aronnax* turned toward the *Nebula*, the last five serpents headed to sea.

24

THE FIRST AUTHORITIES to make it to the beach were MI5, who put the news reports of giant snakes together with the prank call they'd received.

As soon as the *Kekada* rejoined Gabriel and Cora at the *Nebula*, Cora's mask of calm fell away. Gabriel watched it happen. One minute she was resolute, watching the pilots of the Watch disappear from the sonar. And the next, she crumpled.

"Hey." Gabriel took her by the arm. Misty grabbed the other as Peter took the lead. "Come with us."

Misty kept her arm around Cora as Nerissa dropped them off at the beach, where they called an Uber.

Once they were on the road, Cora seemed to perk up. She looked out the window, staring, her head moving, following the shapes of the cars, the streets. "I always wondered what it would be like." She sat back between Misty and Gabriel. "And now I ... get to find out."

When they got out at the little cottage where their families were waiting, Misty and Peter ran toward the door. Gabriel stopped. Smells he was completely unfamiliar with wafted from the place.

Misty looked back. "What is it?"

"I've never been to a Thanksgiving," Gabriel said.

"Well," Peter said, taking Cora's arm, "she hasn't, either."

Peter's mom opened the door. She was wearing a sweater with white flour smudged all over it. "Oh!" She hugged him and ushered the rest inside.

"Who's this?" She was already hurrying back to the kitchen. She grabbed an oven mitt off the counter and opened the oven. Nearby, Misty's parents were busy, her mom tossing an enormous salad, her dad dolloping whipped cream onto a pie. Gabriel smelled butter and cinnamon and bread.

"This is Cora," Gabriel said. "Is it okay if we have a guest?"

"At Thanksgiving you always have guests, or you should," Ms. Kosydar said. "Do we need to call anybody? Sweetie?"

Cora blinked, looking around at her alien surroundings. "No," she said. "No, that's all right." But her voice was thick.

"She can stay with me," Misty said. "I stayed with her in the city we found."

"Found a city," Mr. Jensen said, shaking his head. "Well, I'm glad you guys are home." He looked around. "Close enough."

Cora sniffed as Misty pulled her aside and down to the couch.

"Molly?" Ms. Kosydar called, and Misty's sister came out of another room. "Could you help me with this?" She was hauling out a big metal pan, on which lay a golden-brown turkey. Molly took a pair of pot holders, and Ms. Kosydar showed her where to pick up the pan. Then she called to Peter, "When you said we should stay inland we didn't know what to think."

"Well, it was hard to explain."

"*Giant snakes in the bay* wouldn't do it?" She and Molly set the turkey down. Then she picked a set of keys off the top of the refrigerator, turned to Molly, who really did seem to be Ms. Kosydar's little helper, and said, "Would you run out to the rental car and grab the ladles I bought? I forgot to bring them in."

Molly smiled, took the keys, and came through the archway into the living room. She stopped across the coffee table from the crew. "Are you all right?" she asked. She was looking at Cora, concern crossing her small face.

Cora nodded, and Molly went out.

"I just realized I can't go home." Cora put her hands on her face. "Really can't. I used my own belt to get us into the sub. I fought with Nils. I betrayed the City."

"Minerva betrayed the City," Gabriel said. "If the City was about respecting the sea, what she was planning wasn't the way to do it. Which is why you were right."

"Look," Peter said, "maybe after a while they'll get that. And maybe we can take you back...maybe you can go back."

Ms. Jensen called the four of them. "Guys? You should come sit." Gabriel stood up and saw the table. The flashing silver and the mounds of stuffing. The glistening turkey and the shining cranberries. Pies that sparkled with brushed butter.

"All right," Peter said. "And you've got Tofurkey. How about that." Indeed he pointed at a brown loaf of what Gabriel could only assume was a soy-based imitation meat. He actually didn't particularly care if his food pretended to be meat, but then he thought about the fact that they'd gotten it for him. His face prickled red.

"I just want to say..." Gabriel looked at Ms. Jensen. "We were invited to a thing, an event, today. And Misty was absolutely crazy at the thought that someone would even suggest that we miss this." They all laughed. "And I see why."

"Well, everyone sit," Ms. Kosydar said, carrying a gravy boat. "Where's Molly with the ladles?"

The door opened. Molly called, "Hey! There's someone out here."

The hairs bristled on the back of Gabriel's neck. He looked back with visions of Nils barging in with an army of invaders from the deep.

248

But as Molly turned and held the door wider, they saw that it was Nerissa.

"Oh!" Gabriel got up. Nerissa stood in the doorway with her hands before her, as humble as he'd ever seen her. "This… This is my sister." His heart swelled to see her. She so rarely came on land. And yet she had done it to be with him.

"Hello," Nerissa said. She looked around the room at the friendly faces as Molly took a space next to Misty. Three parents and Molly and the crew looked back at her. "I don't mean to intrude."

"My goodness, no," Mr. Jensen said. He held out his hand, sweeping the table. There was a spot near the end, next to Gabriel. "Please."

Nerissa came to the table and Gabriel pulled out her chair. Misty took the initiative to introduce Nerissa to everyone. As Ms. Jensen ran to grab another place setting, Nerissa whispered to her brother, "Hey. I wanted to show you something."

"What's that?"

She took a tablet out of her pocket and swiveled it around to him. On it were a set of blueprints.

Plans for a ship.

Gabriel felt his heart thump.

OBSCURE II.

"Whoa," Peter said, looking across the table. "Is that what I think it is?"

"We'll look at it later," Nerissa said, and put it away with a wink.

As Ms. Jensen brought her a plate and utensils, Nerissa thanked her. She looked at the parents and laughed lightly. "We're not Americans, so . . . I don't really know how this works."

"Well," Ms. Kosydar said, "everyone does it a little differently. But I think we're going to join hands." They all clasped hands, around the table, Nerissa and Gabriel and Cora, Misty and Molly and Peter, Ms. Kosydar and Mr. Jensen and Ms. Jensen.

"And?" Gabriel asked.

"And one by one, we're going to give thanks."

And so they did.

ACKNOWLEDGMENTS

Here we are at the end of another Young Captain Nemo adventure. Every time I've approached one of these books, it has been to try to explore something about undersea adventure stories that just makes my heart soar. That's why in the first book, our heroes went out on a mission to discover a secret new creature (as in Jules Verne's *20,000 Leagues Under the Sea*), and in the second book, the crew was racing against the clock to find another submarine (as in Tom Clancy's *The Hunt for Red October*). In this book, we explore yet another trope that has always excited me, that of the mysterious undersea kingdom with its own customs and culture, but in a style that would be immediately familiar to the readers. We saw undersea kingdoms like this in such movie serials as *The Phantom Empire* and of course the 1969 film *Captain Nemo and the Underwater City*, starring Robert Ryan. So if you're wondering where all of this is coming from, hit me up on Twitter and I can throw you a bunch more suggestions.

As usual, I've tried to fill the book with places and things that you can look up or even visit. Most of the activity in this book takes place around Cardiff Bay on the coast of Wales. Cardiff has become fairly famous in recent years as the home of such productions as *Doctor Who* and *Torchwood*. It is a place full of rich history, but more than this, it's a place that inspires us, because from a depressed tidal area was born a gorgeous new lake and destination as described in the book. Anything I've gotten wrong, of course, is completely my own fault.

When I set out to write the Young Captain Nemo novels, what I really wanted to do was to give one the impression that even amidst all that is disconcerting and depressing about today's world, there will always be room for those of us who seek to find out what the options are and what we can do next. Young Captain Nemo isn't just a hero to me; rather, he is a sort of alter ego who teaches me to always look for the next thing to do.

Once again, I would like to thank the creative team that makes these books possible, especially my incredibly patient editor, Holly West; designers Katie Klimowicz and

Trisha Previte; Lelia Mander, Ilana Worrell, Lauren Forte, Melanie Sanders, and Veronica Ambrose of the managing editorial and copyediting team at Feiwel & Friends, and, of course, Eric Hibbeler, whose paintings give life to Gabriel Nemo and his friends.

The water is wide, and we will be back around.